## THE AUTHOR

**GABRIELLE ROY** was born in St. Boniface, Manitoba, in 1909. Her parents were part of the large Quebec emigration to western Canada in the late nineteenth century. The youngest of eight children, she studied in a convent school for twelve years, then taught school herself, first in isolated Manitoba villages and later in St. Boniface.

In 1937 Roy travelled to Europe to study drama, and during two years spent in London and Paris she began her writing career. The approaching war forced her to return to Canada, and she settled in Montreal.

Roy's first novel, *The Tin Flute*, ushered in a new era of realism in Quebec fiction with its compassionate depiction of a working-class family in Montreal's Saint-Henri district. Her later fiction often turned for its inspiration to the Manitoba of her childhood and her teaching career.

In 1947 Roy married Dr. Marcel Carbotte, and after a few years in France, they settled in Quebec City, which was to remain their home. Roy complemented her fiction with essays, reflective recollections, and three children's books. Her many honours include three Governor General's Awards, France's Prix Fémina, and Quebec's Prix David.

Gabrielle Roy died in Quebec City, Quebec, in 1983.

STREET OF RICHES

GABRIELLE ROY

TRANSLATED BY
HENRY BINSSE

AFTERWORD BY
MIRIAM WADDINGTON

*Rue Deschambault*
Original edition copyright © 1955 by Gabrielle Roy

*Street of Riches*
Translated edition copyright © 1957 by Gabrielle Roy
Afterword copyright © 1991 by Miriam Waddington

First New Canadian Library edition 1991.
This New Canadian Library edition 2008.

This book was first published in English in 1957 by McClelland & Stewart.

**Library and Archives Canada Cataloguing in Publication**

Roy, Gabrielle, 1909-1983
        Street of riches / Gabrielle Roy ; translated by Henry Binsse ; with an afterword by Miriam Waddington.

(New Canadian library)
Translation of: Rue Deschambault.
First published in English: 1957.
ISBN 978-0-7710-7782-1

        I. Binsse, Harry Lorin, 1905- II. Title. III. Series.

PS8535.095R813 2008        C843'.54        C2007-906238-5


We acknowledge the financial support of the Government of Canada through the Book Publishing Industry Development Program and that of the Government of Ontario through the Ontario Media Development Corporation's Ontario Book Initiative. We further acknowledge the support of the Canada Council for the Arts and the Ontario Arts Council for our publishing program.

Typeset in Garamond by M&S, Toronto
Printed and bound in the United States of America

McClelland & Stewart Ltd.
75 Sherbourne Street
Toronto, Ontario
M5A 2P9
www.mcclelland.com/NCL


        2   3   4   5      12   11   10   09

# CONTENTS

## THE TWO NEGROES

When he built our home, my father took as model the only other house then standing on the brief length of Rue Deschambault – still unencumbered by any sidewalk, as virginal as a country path stretching through thickets of wild roses and, in April, resonant with the music of frogs. Maman was pleased with the street, with the quiet, with the good, pure air there, for the children, but she objected to the servile copying of our neighbor's house, which was luckily not too close to ours. This neighbor, a Monsieur Guilbert, was a colleague of my father's at the Ministry of Colonization and his political enemy to boot, for Papa had remained passionately faithful to Laurier's memory, while Monsieur Guilbert, when the Conservative party came into power, had become a turncoat. Over this the two men quarreled momentously. My father would return home after one of these set-tos chewing on his little clay pipe. He would inform my mother: "I'm through. I'll never set foot there again. The old jackass, with his Borden government!"

My mother concurred: "Certainly. You'd do far better to stay home than go looking for an argument wherever you stick your nose."

Yet no more than my father could forgo his skirmishes with Monsieur Guilbert could she forgo her own with our neighbor's wife.

This lady was from St. Hyacinth, in the Province of Quebec, and she made much of it. But above all she had a way of extolling her own children which, while lauding them, seemed to belittle Maman's. "My Lucien is almost too conscientious," she would say. "The Fathers tell me they have never seen a child work so hard."

My mother would retort: "Only yesterday the Fathers told me again that my Gervais is so intelligent everything comes to him effortlessly; and apparently that's not too good a thing, either."

My mother was most skillful in parrying what she called Madame Guilbert's "thrusts." Despite all this – or perhaps because of it – our two families could scarcely get along without each other.

Often of an evening my mother would go out on the open porch in front of our big house and say to my sister Odette, "Supper is ready. Run over and tell your father; he's still at the Guilberts'. Bring him back before any argument begins."

Odette would sally forth across the field. When she reached the Guilberts', there my father would be, his pipe clamped between his teeth, leaning against our neighbor's gate and chatting peaceably with Monsieur Guilbert about rosebushes, apple trees, and asparagus. So long as the two men were on such subjects, there was no need for alarm; and here Monsieur Guilbert was willing enough to accept my father's views, since he granted that my father knew more about gardening than he did. Then Odette would espy Gisèle's face at one of the upstairs windows. Gisèle would call out, "Wait for me, Odette; I'm coming down. I want to show you my tatting."

In those days they were both fanatically devoted to piano playing and to a sort of lacemaking that involved the use of a shuttle and was, if my memory serves me well, called tatting.

Then my mother would send my brother Gervais to see what on earth could be keeping my Father and Odette over there. At the field's edge, Gervais would encounter his classmate Lucien Guilbert, and the latter would entice my brother behind an ancient barn to smoke a cigarette; needless to say, Madame Guilbert always maintained that it was Gervais who had induced Lucien to indulge this bad habit.

Out of patience, Maman would ship me off to corral them all. But I would chance to meet the Guilberts' dog, and we would start playing in the tall grass; among us all, now at loggerheads, now so closely knit, I think that only I and the Guilbert dog were always of the same temper.

At last my mother would tear off her apron and come marching along the footpath to reprimand us. "My supper's been ready for an hour now!"

Madame Guilbert would then appear on her own porch and graciously exclaim, "Dear, dear! Do stay here for supper, seeing as you're all here anyway."

For Madame Guilbert, when you yielded her her full rights to superiority and distinction, was a most amiable person. Still, it was difficult to avoid, throughout an entire evening, the subject of Sir Wilfrid Laurier, or to settle once and for all which boy had induced the other to smoke; and the consequence was that often enough we came home from these kindly visits quite out of humor with the Guilberts.

Such was our situation – getting along together happily enough, I avow – when the unknown quite fantastically entered our lives, and brought with it relationships more difficult, yet how vastly more interesting!

## II

Neither family in those days was well off; there were times when sheer necessity made us keenly aware of its harsh grasp, and my mother had acquired the habit of saying, "We must make our minds up to rent a room. The house is so large we'll scarcely notice it." My mother, however, began to be fearful of the shady character or the humble workingman who would appear every evening and come into our home filthy from his toil.

Whenever she spoke of this, she seemed so obviously to feel Madame Guilbert's disapproval weighing upon her that we all laughed a little at Maman; for, on other occasions, she was well able to hold her head high and announce that, "as for her, her conscience was clear . . ." or that "she didn't care a fig for what others might say. . . ."

Her lodger was becoming more and more of an ideal being. The fellow must go to bed early, never touch hard liquor, be quiet, neither too young nor too old . . . and if possible be distinguished.

So often had she heard that adjective on Madame Guilbert's lips that my mother had no use for it, but she strove all the same to twist its meaning toward what to her constituted true distinction. Yet where would one find this exemplary being who would give us money and not cause us the least trifling annoyance – who, to suit Maman's taste, would be at once invisible and distinguished?

Whereupon, my oldest brother, Robert, arrived home one day bubbling with excitement. Like Horace, the Guilberts' first-born, he worked in Her Majesty's service, aboard the mail car on the Winnipeg-Edmonton run. He was full of life and exuberance. Madame Guilbert was constantly drawing the contrast between our Robert and her Horace, a lad with so keen an eye to the future, who saved his money and never touched a drop of Scotch. . . .

"I've found the very roomer you need," Robert told Maman. "Just perfect!"

"Really?"

"Yes, indeed."

"He doesn't drink?"

"Not a drop."

"Doesn't smoke?"

"Just one cigar at Christmas."

"Dear me!" exclaimed Maman, who paled to find fate thus taking her at her own words.

"Better still," added Robert, "this chap will occupy his room here only a day or two each week, but he'll pay for it in full. . . ."

"And the rest of the time . . . where will he be?" Maman asked.

"Now here, now there," Robert replied, laughing at Maman's expression. "Sometimes in Vancouver . . . or Edmonton . . . But don't worry; he is a most honorable employee of the Canadian Pacific."

"Therefore . . . quite presentable?"

"The looks of a president . . . and devout as well," said Robert.

"A president and devout! What's his name?"

"Jackson."

"English?"

"He is English-speaking, all right," Robert replied. . . . "But, truth to tell – and here's the one small shadow on the picture, if I may put it that way – Jackson is a Negro."

"A Negro! No, indeed! Never in the world!"

My mother had cast a glance toward the house next door. And it was so much as though she had said aloud "Whatever would Madame Guilbert think of it!" that we all deliberately and gravely looked in the same direction.

Nonetheless, my mother reconciled herself to the idea; basically, I think, her curiosity was the strongest of her feelings. Heavens, she was as curious, almost, as Madame Guilbert! Not long after, I recall, there came a brilliant June day, and all of us were stationed at the windows – I way up in the attic – to see our Negro arrive.

A little earlier, Maman had murmured, "All the same, I'd almost rather he had first arrived at night!"

In broad daylight, along our tiny and little-frequented street, and with the sun shining bright, the fact is that this large, handsome black man, clad wholly in black and equipped with his little porter's satchel, was highly conspicuous.

He looked happy as he drew up in front of our house; at a glance he took in the three small apple trees in bloom, the wide porch with its row of rocking chairs, the fresh look of the paint, and even my diminutive countenance staring down at him. For my benefit he rolled round the incredible whites of his eyes. I rushed headlong downstairs to see how Maman would welcome the Negro. And Maman, in her embarrassment, perhaps, at extending a Negro a proper greeting, stretched out her hand, then half withdrew it, while making a sort of reverential bow and saying to him, "Welcome, Mr. Jackson, from C.P.R., *n'est-ce pas?*"

Then she showed him to his room. A little later she came back downstairs: at last it was over with – our Negro was under our roof. We could consider and attend to other matters, as my mother put it. Yet during the whole livelong day, the Negro up there seemingly did not budge. This silence on his part constantly forced him back upon our attention. "Perhaps he's asleep . . ." one of us would suggest. Or, again, "He's reading his Bible. . . ." With a sigh, Agnès said, "He's lonely . . . maybe. . . ." My mother frowned. "Still and all, we can't urge him this soon to come down into the kitchen. . . ." Occasionally my mother would take a look through a window facing their house to see what was going on at the Guilberts'. There, also, only silence.

"I do wish she'd come over!" Maman exclaimed. "I'm certain that she saw our Negro arrive, and that she's at her window wondering who he can be."

And, indeed, at about four o'clock, Madame Guilbert sedately – she would don her hat whether she were merely dropping across the field between us or were on her way to church – came to get the news. Once installed in a chair, she took her usual circuitous path toward satisfying her curiosity, carefully avoiding as ill-bred any direct question.

"So?" she remarked.

Maman knew how to keep her dangling. "My my," said she, "how hot it is already! And only the eighteenth of June! . . ."

"It surely is hot," agreed Madame Guilbert. "And speaking of that, haven't your summer guests begun to arrive? I thought I saw someone go into your house with a small suitcase. . . . I was just hanging some curtains. . . ."

"Yes, a guest of a sort," said Maman. "I made up my mind to take a lodger."

"Oh! So that's it! You know," Madame Guilbert explained, "I must have had the sun in my eyes . . . when that person . . . your lodger, I mean . . . turned in at the end of the street. . . . For a moment I thought I saw a Negro."

"Perhaps the sun was in your eyes," said my mother politely, "but you saw correctly all the same: it was, indeed, a Negro."

And then Maman took the initiative; comfortably she settled into a wholly new role. "I could have rented my room a hundred . . . two hundred times to some white person," said my mother. "There's no lack of whites in these parts. . . . But that's just it; I realized that it was more humane, more Christian – if you will – to take this poor Negro whom certain persons – you know what I mean – would refuse to treat like one of their own kind. For indeed – yes or no –" Maman asked, "has a Negro a soul?"

At first overwhelmed, Madame Guilbert finally regained her capacity to give tit for tat.

"Tsck, tsck . . ." she indicated her incredulity. "Are you going to try to make me believe that you have installed a black person in our midst out of philanthropy?"

"No . . . maybe not . . ." said my mother with a gracious smile. "But I must admit it, Madame Guilbert: now that I have a Negro, I wish I had accepted him from the outset out of pure philanthropy, as you put it, so deeply am I aware that I acted as I ought. . . ."

For the moment, Madame Guilbert gave every indication of looking upon my mother with benevolence. Then, putting her hat back on her head, she remarked offhandedly, as though without the least ulterior motive, "True enough . . . it must be a paying proposition to have a roomer one or two days a week . . . but who will pay you for all seven, I presume!"

Maman, who, in point of fact, had taken the Negro only to ease our circumstances a little, continued smiling, thoroughly pleased with herself. And she remarked for our benefit, "That a good deed should bear fruit – what is so astounding about that? It's no more than natural."

### III

Dear Negro! He had the most generous soul in the world, and it was indeed thanks to him that, without their causing us too much suffering, we survived serious money troubles that summer, which turned out hot, sluggish, and sleepy, as summer always should be.

On the evening of his second stay with us, the Negro came down from his room. He reached the bottom of the stairs, and, with his face close against the screen door, he inquired in his deep voice – we were all sitting on the porch, getting a breath of air – whether he might join us. He said that on his Vancouver train the heat had been appalling, and all he wanted was to sit on the stoop. Mother assigned him to a chair. Then from his pocket the Negro extracted the first of the many gifts he was to offer us. It was a pair of white gloves; he presented them to Agnès, the shyest and the gentlest of my sisters. We were all a trifle embarrassed; but, then, not to accept this first gift from our Negro would have hurt him too much. And besides, Agnès had every intention of keeping the gloves.

Thus it went. Each time he stayed with us, our Negro never failed to come take his place on the porch. My mother had planted stock all round, and its flowers exhaled their fullest scent at night. Through the Eau de Cologne and cheap powder of which he reeked, the Negro must have gathered a few breaths of this more delicate perfume from the living blossoms.

On such evenings, rolling his big eyes, his thumbs stuck in his vest pockets, he would say happily, "Smell so goo-ood!"

He would add, "It's fine not to be rollin' across Canada."

And he would pull out of his pocket a white silk scarf for my father, then white silk stockings, for Agnès again . . . almost always something white. As for me, I had become his French teacher. He would point out some object for me – a tree, a house, a chair. I would say *arbre, maison, chaise*. . . . Then the Negro would thrust his hand in his pocket and bring out a ten-cent piece which he would slip into the slot of my penny bank. I was paid for each three words. I had glimpses of the fortune I would make teaching French.

Meanwhile, the Guilberts were having serious money trouble. Monsieur Guilbert had retired because of age; the large house, so similar to our own, was mortgaged. The children who were still at school required heavy expenditures. When she realized how distracted her neighbor was, my mother tried to help without wounding Madame Guilbert's pride. One day she sent her a quantity of hare, of which she claimed to have far too great a supply, and on another occasion, when we had received a dozen chickens from one of my country uncles, Maman insisted upon Madame Guilbert's accepting half of them, assuring her that our family could not eat them quickly enough, that they would spoil. And my father no longer reviled Monsieur Guilbert as a sellout to the Borden government or called him an old jackass, but only an impoverished fool.

One day my mother suggested to her neighbor, "Why wouldn't you take in a lodger yourself, Madame Guilbert? There's nothing dishonorable about it. . . ."

"Yes, I've thought of it," sighed Madame Guilbert, "but to bring a stranger into our homes, to mingle with our growing boys and young girls – a strange person – is a serious business, as you know . . . ."

"Yes, it's serious," Maman agreed, "but strangers are rarely as strange as one might think . . . ."

"I put an advertisement in the paper," admitted Madame Guilbert. "There was no response. . . . Times are hard, you know . . . roomers are scarce. . . . Our little street isn't very well known. . . ."

Then she asked, "All in all, you're pleased with your Negro?"

"Pleased? I couldn't be more pleased! Just imagine, Madame Guilbert, he makes his own bed!"

"That's easily understood," Madame Guilbert remarked with some asperity. "A *porter!* A man who makes up other people's beds! It would be the last straw – don't you think? – if he didn't make his own!"

"Yes, but, search as I will, I can't find a thing to put to rights in his room," said my mother; "not even a necktie to pick up, or a pair of socks . . . I assure you. Madame Guilbert, Negroes seem to me the neatest and cleanest men in the world. . . ."

"About their persons as well?" asked Madame Guilbert, with a slight tightening of her nostrils.

My mother laughed. "I'm afraid that's his one fault. He's forever taking baths. He uses up every bit of our hot water . . . ."

"But does he keep his place?"

"Keep his place? What do you mean?" Maman exclaimed. "Certainly he keeps his place . . . just as each of us, Madame Guilbert, has his station in life – you'll agree? – not as rich as some . . . not as poor as others. . . ."

In those days on Rue Deschambault we lived as though we were in the country. But along Rue Desmeurons, where our street ended, and which itself was none too built up, a yellow trolley car passed by every fifteen minutes. It discharged very few passengers for Deschambault: my father most days at about six, returning from his office; or else Horace and my brother Robert, who returned together on Thursdays from their travels; and our Negro, of course, who always arrived on Fridays. But on a certain Friday it was not a single Negro who stepped down from the tram; there were two of them, clad alike in black, each with his little bag. One of the Negroes, ours, stopped at our gate; the other, after waving his hand at his companion and calling out, "So long, Buddy!" went on to the Guilberts', whistling as he walked.

It was my mother's turn to be on pins and needles; and since Madame Guilbert did not appear, she found herself obliged to go over for the news.

"Yes, indeed," Madame Guilbert told her, "my Horace has known this Negro a long while; they travel on the same train. He's a steady, quiet Negro, very well-bred. . . ."

"Like mine, exactly," said Maman.

"After all, a C.P.R. employee, just like our sons," continued Madame Guilbert.

But my mother was counting on too easy a triumph, and Madame Guilbert reminded her: "The moment there was already one Negro on our street . . . it wasn't too serious a matter to bring in another. Once the example had been set! . . ."

Mother came home a trifle put out. "Anyway," she assured us, "our Negro is infinitely superior to Madame Guilbert's; hers is less well-built, less erect in his bearing. . . ." And, as though to establish for good her neighbor's bad faith, Maman prophesied: "You'll see that now Madame Guilbert is going to claim she has a better Negro than ours! You'll see!"

Which is exactly what happened.

However, without the least shadow of doubt, the Guilbert's Negro was the less dark in color of the two. And it was precisely this – can you believe it? – that gave Madame Guilbert ground for her pride, since she would observe, "I really believe that he's no more than a mulatto!"


IV

In the meantime our Negro gave us lessons in kindness. For hours on end in the evening he would hold upon his large outstretched hands skeins of wool which Maman wound into balls. Agnès wore her white gloves even while sitting on the porch. Maman crunched candies brought from Vancouver. My penny bank had been filled, emptied, and was in process of being filled again. They say I dogged our Negro's every foot-step, penny bank in hand – but I think that was an exaggeration. In the first place, if the Negro gave me the large price of ten cents per lesson, it was because my bank was made in the style of the money containers used by trolley conductors, and allowed only dimes to pass through its slot. Besides, it could not be opened as long as it was not full. In any case, Maman was very wrong to reproach me, for when my bank was again full, she again borrowed from me all its contents – five dollars. I was the ant of the fable, save that from time to time I came to the assistance of the grasshopper. Despite these repeated loans, I ever labored to refill my bank with an eye to a purchase of my own. And then it was that my sister Odette started to be my serious competitor . . . so serious that she succeeded in distracting the Negro completely from his French lessons.

She was later to become a nun; she detested men and, before renouncing the world and herself, she had the soul of a revolutionist. The idea of injustice in the world made her tighten her lips; merely having read in a newspaper that a poor tramp had been found shivering with cold in a park aroused in Odette a smoldering anger against the whole city. Her thin-drawn nostrils were constantly pulsing with indignation. Assuredly she was not made for the world; she was lovely to look at and, having at last given up her tatting, she was constantly playing a certain one of Rachmaninoff's preludes. There was a portion of this piece, in vibrant chords, that she said gave expression to the rebellion of the wretches in Siberia. I was crazy about this rebellion in music. Wherever I might be, under the apple trees or farther off at play with my little Gauthier friends, the moment I heard the rumble of the march toward Siberia, I left everything, rushed into the parlor, and squatted on the rug near the piano. I watched Odette's swelling nostrils, her tight-drawn lips. I would ask, "The rebellion's coming?" Without stopping or even looking at me, Odette would give me a nod of affirmation; then with a movement of her hips she would push the piano bench back a little so as to have a longer reach for the terrible moments to come.

Our Negro must also have felt the spell of this music. He came down the stairs gently, very gently. He stopped at about the eighth step, on the turn; he sat down; between the slats of the banister he could catch a glimpse of Odette, who in those days had a mass of very fine blonde hair which her movements at the piano and her agitation scattered over her forehead and down her neck in golden strands. One evening Odette lifted her head; she saw the Negro, his face between the bars of the stairway. Concluding, perhaps with truth and certainly with remorse, that she had kept him shut away from her music just as were the exiles of her prelude from the kingdom of the czars, my sister, pointing to an armchair, with the utmost graciousness invited the Negro into the parlor. And in his honor she played Rachmaninoff's prelude all over again, from the beginning.

It was so clearly understood among us that Odette had no inclination toward young men, that she was not cut out for them, that no one thought of being astonished at seeing her with the Negro. Moreover, he treated her with a respect that made appear insignificant the gallantries and compliments of bachelors with an eye to marriage. And Odette, resolved as she was upon renunciation, seemed greatly to like being the object of such great concern. In the evening, after the music, she and the Negro would walk together in front of the house. They talked about Africa. Doubtless in the hope of pleasing my sister, our Negro tried to bring back old memories, vaguely handed down in the Jackson family, of slaves on the auction block, of raids by rapacious men, of poor black folk taken by surprise in their straw-hut villages. . . .

"Yes . . . Miss . . . all that must have happened once upon a time . . ." the Negro would say, shortening his stride to keep in step with Odette.

V

On these same evenings, so soft, so perfumed – for in those days along Rue Deschambault there were untouched stands of clover and wild hay, which a man sent by the city would cut down with a scythe only at summer's end – on these evenings which were summer itself, my mother would often "fetch" Madame Guilbert for a little walk. The two women strolled back and forth along the short length of road in front of Madame Guilbert's house. And everything went well enough between them, except when they chanced to speak of their Negroes; they were relentlessly determined to settle which of them had the better of the two.

"Mine," Maman would say, "has refinement, I assure you, and tact."

"However that may be, mine has enough of those qualities," Madame Guilbert would reply, "to know his place and stay there."

"Do you mean by that, Madame Guilbert," my mother would ask, "that you have the heart to condemn your poor Negro to remain in his room during this heat? . . . People who suffer so much from the heat! . . . and are so sensitive at heart! . . ."

Once while they were thus chatting as they walked, they became aware, though at a considerable distance, of a couple strolling in front of our house.

"Now," said Madame Guilbert, raising her eyes and shading them with her hand against the setting sun, "who on earth is that man out walking with Odette?"

"A man with Odette would certainly be a great surprise to me!" said Maman.

At the same time, though, my mother pushed Madame Guilbert a little with her elbow, trying to make her turn about: but since this tactic was unsuccessful, she sought to call her attention to the tallness of the wild hay, to a low-flying bird. Madame Guilbert kept marching straight toward our house. She now had a better view of our part of the street, and in horror she exclaimed, "Do you know who it is with Odette, my poor friend? Your Negro! I'm sure of it! It's not yet dark enough for me not to make out that dusky face. . . ."

"In that case, never complain of your eyesight," said Maman; "it is still better than mine."

Then, quite calmly, as though upon reflection the event was to her advantage, she said, "Indeed, it's quite possible that Odette should be out walking with the Negro; the child has such a big heart!"

"What!" exclaimed Madame Guilbert. "I tell you that your daughter is out walking with a Negro for any and all to see, and you simply say, 'Oh!'"

"That's exactly it," said my mother, "in plain sight of everyone. . . ." Then she went on, "In plain sight of very few persons, I'll have you notice, Madame Guilbert; in plain sight of just precisely the two of us."

All the same, Maman was annoyed. Cutting short her walk, she returned to rebuke Odette a little. "That you should chat with the Negro on the porch, in the parlor – well enough! But do you have to do it before the eyes of the whole neighborhood?"

"The neighborhood!" repeated my sister, tightening her lips. "What neighborhood?"

Now Madame Guilbert's Negro was a small, quiet man, formerly from Alabama, who also was attracted to music. Gisèle in those days played four-handed pieces with Odette; when she was left in the lurch by my sister, who now sought the Negro's company, she began endlessly repeating, until well into the evening, a composition by Schumann, which I seem to remember was called "The Well-Beloved." While her mother and mine sauntered in front of the Guilbert house, Gisèle played for their Negro, who in his turn, step by step, had finally achieved the parlor. Maybe Madame Guilbert suspected it, but probably she preferred to know that they were in the house rather than on the porch, in plain sight of everyone.

However this may be, when Madame Guilbert stopped sulking at Maman and came over one evening to "pick her up" for a little stroll, she would not hear of going in her own direction, preferring our end, which she suddenly said was more airy and less unsociable.

So it was in front of our house that they promenaded back and forth. At the other end of the street there likewise passed to and fro a man and a woman who seemed well matched in height and gait; dusk was falling; Maman could not make out the faces of this happy-seeming couple. Around the Guilberts' the shade of night fell sooner than it did around our house because of the heavy thickets surrounding theirs.

"So your Gisèle has a suitor?" asked Maman, with a touch of envy. For though she seemed to approve Odette's keeping young men at arm's length, actually it pained Maman, especially when she saw Gisèle's beaux going up our street with little bunches of flowers in their hands.

"She has no lack of admirers," said Madame Guilbert proudly. "I assure you, dear friend, it makes no sense; when it isn't one, it's another. . . . It's a good thing for a girl to be popular, but, as I keep telling Gisèle, 'Daughter, if you encourage too many of them, you'll set them all at each other's ears. . . .'"

"And God alone knows what might happen then . . ." Maman continued, cheerful once again.

"What's more," said Madame Guilbert, "I find her behaviour more natural than your Odette's. Odette's rather pretty, you know; I think she'd go far if she did not feel herself obliged to chase all the men away . . . except, of course, your Negro. . . ."

"But a Negro," said my mother mysteriously, "does not

turn a girl away from a vocation . . . quite the opposite. . . . Come to think of it, though, I do believe it's the first time I've ever seen this beau of Gisèle's. . . . Can it be a new one? . . ."

"I didn't know she was expecting someone this evening," Madame Guilbert admitted. "Let's see, who could it be? . . . There's Dr. Tremblay, who's crazy about her. . . . And the notary. . ."

"This evening, however," said Maman, "I think it's the Negro. . . ."

"My Negro! With Gisèle! In plain sight! . . ."

"I haven't got my glasses," said Maman, "but from here, it looks very much like a black face – or rather, brown, since your Negro is only a mulatto. . . ."

She had no time to add anything further; Madame Guilbert was on her way toward the other end of the street, and in her haste she beat her arms a little, as though they were a pair of wings.

A little later, severed from his companion, the Guilberts' Negro came to the parlor to join forces with ours, who was singing to Odette's accompaniment. Then Gisèle appeared and sat beside my sister on the piano bench, and the two young girls supported with four hands the voices of the two Negroes, who launched into lovely improvised harmonies; one voice as deep as the night, the other no deeper than the dusk, they poured out of all our open windows, they rolled forth, mingled with the glints of the moonlight, and made the grasses quiver.

On the porch, my mother sat rocking in her chair.

Alas, it was at the very moment when our lives might have become who knows how much more interesting that our Negroes were summoned away by their sleeping cars, one to make the run between Halifax and Montreal, the other, I believe, obliged to return to Calgary.

And for a long time, for years even, Rue Deschambault missed its Negroes.

# PETITE MISÈRE

Shortly after I came into the world, my father, because I was of frail health or because he himself – then old and sick – had too great a pity for life, dubbed me "Petite Misère" – "Little Miss Misery." Even when, stroking my hair, he used the name affectionately, it annoyed me and made me unhappy, as though it foreordained me, because of him, to suffering. I bridled and said within myself, "Oh no! I am not misery. Never shall I be like you!"

But one day he hurled the hateful name at me in anger. I don't even know any longer what can have deserved such an explosion; probably some mere trifle; my father went through long periods of dark moodiness, when he lacked all patience and seemed overwhelmed with regrets – perhaps also with too heavy responsibilities. Then, from time to time, a mere peal of laughter, breaking in upon him, penetrating him in the midst of his somber thoughts, aroused in him an outburst of irritation. Later on I understood that, constantly fearing for us both the least and the worst of evils, he especially wanted to put us early on guard against too great a yearning for happiness.

His distorted features, on this particular occasion, had seemed terrifying to me. He threatened me with his upraised hand; but, powerless to make up his mind to strike me, he hurled at me as an everlasting reproach: "Oh! Why did I ever have any children!"

Parents may think that such words, well beyond the understanding of children, do them no harm; but precisely because they are only half intelligible to them, children ponder them and make of them a torture.

I fled; I ran up to my attic, where, face against the floor, I tore my nails over the rough boards and tried to dig my way into them that I might die. Pressing my nose and mouth against their wood, I attempted to prevent myself from breathing. I believed that one could stop breathing at will, and thus leave evil behind, whenever one wants to, because it is evil.

Hours passed, and I turned over on my back; my face-down position was really too uncomfortable.

And then, through the attic window, which was just in my line of vision, I beheld the sky. It was a windy June day . . . and very handsome, very white clouds began to pass before my eyes. It seemed to me that the clouds were displaying themselves for my sole benefit. Over the roof, so close to me, the wind whistled. Even at that age I loved the wind in high places, attacking neither men nor trees, doing no harm, a simple traveler who whistles as he goes. Two large elms planted by my father thrust their highest branches to the edge of my window; by stretching my neck a little, I could watch them sway; and that, too, must have been for me alone, since I was the only person perched high enough to espy the upper branches of our elms.

Then, more than ever, I wanted to die, because of the emotion that a mere tree was able to arouse in me . . . sweet, traitorous emotion, revealing to me that sorrow has eyes the better to see how lovely is this world!

For a moment my attention was wholly enthralled by the sight of a spider lowering itself toward me from a ceiling rafter, at the tip of its silken path. Because of it, I forgot to cry. But strengthened by having eluded me for a few moments, my sorrow returned and filled all my soul, while at the same time I studied through my tears this poor, tiny insect life, which I could cut short with a tap of my finger.

And I said to myself: "My father wanted no part of me. No one wanted any part of me. I should not have come into the world." (Occasionally I had heard my mother referring to some poor woman already burdened with children and in ill health, who had just brought another into the world, remark with a sigh, "It's hard, but that is duty. What can you do? She certainly must do her duty!") That day I dug the word from my memories, seized upon it, and, not yet aware of the terrible meaning it contained, I repeated to myself, "A child of duty! I am a child of duty!" And the very sound of this word sufficed to make me weep anew, for sorrows I did not yet know.

Then I rediscovered the blue sky, sailing past the window. Why did the sky seem to me so beautiful that evening that never since, in any portion of the world, have I seen any like it? Was it because it was so indifferent toward me, who looked upon it?

As I was about to begin weeping once more, I heard steps resound along the hall on the second floor, beneath my attic. Then the door at the foot of the stairs opened. A voice – my mother's voice – called out: "The table is set; supper is ready. Enough sulking – come eat."

Despite everything, I was hungry, and that very fact, the shame of being tempted by food in the midst of my sorrow, made me deny my hunger and assert that I could not eat, that I never should be able to eat again.

At the foot of the stairs my mother said to me, "Well, if you want to sulk, sulk . . . but later on you won't find anything left to eat."

And she moved away with a resilient, still-youthful step.

Later my brother came to the foot of the stairs to cry out to me that he was going fishing in the little river . . . would I go with him? . . . make up my mind! He was not referring to the Red, our valley's important river, but to our small Seine, a narrow watercourse that twisted its way onward like a snake between thickets filled with rose haws, a tiny river buried in the grass, muddy, secret, of little danger to us, even were we to plunge into it headfirst . . . my pretty river, green as cats' eyes!

It was very difficult for me to resist, but once again the idea of joy being possible in a life corrupt with sorrow made me rebuff my brother and cry out that I wanted to be alone.

He also moved away at a rapid pace; I heard him trot down the length of the hall and then gallop down the main stairs leading to the lower floor of the house.

Then there was a silence.

Later still the little Gauthiers, my cherished playmates, all three perched on their plank fence which separated our two properties – though I do recall there was also a vague field between them – kept calling me for a long while. As was our custom, they intoned their summonses to the bird tune of "Fred – er – ick – hast – thou – seen – me." But at exactly the same time, the bird itself was likewise singing. I had to make a real effort to distinguish between its brief phrase of song and the chanting of my friends: "Chris – tine – will – you – come – and – play? At – store – keep – ing – come – and – play? At – bear – train – ing – come – and – play?" At last they varied their recitative a bit; because this was the game I liked the best and because by this means they hoped they might coax me out of the house, they called out plainly, "Come and let's play funerals!"

With that, I could not master the desire to look at them; I drew close to the edge of the window, and I saw them below; all three in a row on the high fence. Yet suddenly reflecting that they were children better loved by their parents than I was by mine, I quickly ducked my head before they could discover me, since, in an obstinate effort to find me, their small faces were scanning all the windows of our house. I turned around, lay down on my back, and stared at the dismal ceiling.

For a good while longer, without catching a glimpse of me anywhere, the dear children called me, in all their youthful despair at seeing so fine a summer evening lost for play. They were still calling me when it was almost dark. Their mother told them to come in and go to bed. I heard their protests and then their mother's insistent voice. But before giving me up, the three of them lined up on the fence cried out very loud, and with how deep a regret: "Good – night – Chris – ti – ne! Are – you – dead – Chris – tine? So – long – Chris – ti – nette!"

Now in the attic window the sky was dark. And my sorrow was reborn, but far more mysterious and unknown. I felt as though it were the future – the whole, long, terrible future of a child – that weighed upon me . . . and I cried in broken sobs, without knowing exactly why. Perhaps because I sensed within me, as among adults, enough cowardice to resign myself to life as it is . . . and perhaps life held me even more firmly in its grasp through curiosity.

I could still hear on the floors below certain sounds that informed me of the goings and comings in the house. Doors slammed. On the porch and then on our narrow cement path I heard my mother's footsteps, in her new shoes. True, this evening she was supposed to play cards at some friends'. She was in a hurry; her feet seemed to run . . . and I was miserable that -- this evening -- she could leave with a free heart to indulge herself in anything so futile as card playing.

The night seemed to rise toward me from the dark floors below. The big house was now wholly silent . . . maybe empty. . . . And my sorrow was beyond bearing, abandoned by all save by myself, save by my solitary concern -- far too young, far too weak to understand that sorrow; and without any longer knowing its cause, I wept for sorrow itself, which is perhaps no more than a child alone.

Then my ear close to the floor heard the dragging, the overburdened tread of my father.

Gently he pulled open the door at the foot of the stairs. There he remained for a long while, without speaking. Perhaps he thought that I did not know he was standing with one foot raised to take the first step. But I could hear his breathing . . . and maybe he could hear mine, so poignant was the silence between us.

At last he called out: "Little one! Petite Misère!"

Oh, how my throat tightened! Never after did I ever feel such a knot, drawn tight to the point of choking me. And it is possibly a good thing while very young to have suffered a terrible sorrow, for afterward sorrow no longer has the power really to astound us.

My old father tried again: "Child!"

Then, since I still gave no answer, my father said to me, "You must be hungry."

And later on, after another silence, he said to me, so sadly that even today, finding its way amid memories as crowded as a forest, the exact tone of my father's voice comes back to me: "I've made a rhubarb pie. . . . It's still hot. . . . Would you like to eat some?"

It's beyond me! Ever since that day, rhubarb pie has never tempted me; but before then, it seems I adored it, even though I was sick every time I ate any. That was why my mother made it only very rarely, and when – rarely – she served one, she would forbid me to take more than one tiny little piece. So, then, my father must have taken advantage of my mother's being out that evening . . . and I could see him rolling up his sleeves, searching for the flour, for the lard – never, indeed, could he succeed in laying his hand on anything around the house – lighting the stove, keeping an eye on the pie as it baked. . . . How could I have uttered an answer! What was the sorrow that all evening had kept me from my usual games compared to the sorrow which now held me in its grip! Was it then the same with sorrow as with the mysterious paths in my book of the *Thousand and One Nights*, where each led on to a broader avenue and disclosed ever-widening vistas?

I heard my father sigh. So slowly did he close the door that I barely was aware of the click of the latch. He went away.

Those slow, disheartened footsteps!

And yet I waited a few minutes, a long time it seemed to me. Then I smoothed out my wrinkled clothes. I patted my cheeks to remove the marks of my tears; and with the hem of my dress I tried to repair the smudges thus left on my face.

I went down, stopping at each step.

The table in our large kitchen was laid as though for a feast . . . a very sorry feast, for on the white cloth there was placed, at the center, only the pie, and at either end, far re-moved from each other, our two plates.

We took our places, my father and I, without having as yet exchanged so much as a glance.

Then my father pushed toward me the pie he had cut beforehand into such huge pieces that abruptly I burst into fresh tears. But at the same time I began to taste it.

Often during halts on his rough trips through lands being opened to colonization, when he had gone to settle immigrants there, my father had improvised his own meals over glowing embers under the stars of the prairies, and from those days he had cherished the illusion – certainly linked to nostalgia for the open spaces and the purity of that life – of being skilled in the kitchen. My mother, however, said that my father's pies were lead.

And this indeed was leaden fare that I valiantly strove to swallow.

Our eyes met. I saw that the mouthful my father had taken was not going down any more easily.

And how keenly then, through my own poor child's sorrow, did I gain a notion of my father's so much weightier sadness, the heaviness of life itself: that indigestible nutriment which this evening, as though it were forever, my father proffered me!

That night I was very sick with a serious attack of indigestion. My mother, having no inkling of what had taken place between the aged man and his Petite Misère, showered my father with reproaches. "To have her eat pie at ten o'clock at night! Have you lost your mind?"

With a sad smile and without pleading any excuse, he bowed his head; and, later, when he came to bring me a dose of medicine, his face was suffused with such grief that, often, I think it immortal.

## MY PINK HAT

I had had jaundice, and Maman, to hasten my recovery, bought me a pink hat. Most likely she tried to make me agree to one of a different color – I was still bright yellow from my illness – but it was pink I wanted. And, laughing a bit, Maman finally yielded.

My best dress to go with this candy-pink hat was of a rough mottled tweed, black and white, with a vivid red collar. None the less, it was thus accoutered that I was to go on my first trip all by myself. Maman was sending me to the country to recapture my normal coloring and my health, and she could not herself leave the family. But on the train she found an aged Gray Nun to whom she entrusted me.

"Are you going as far as Notre Dame de Lourdes?" she asked the Gray Nun.

The Gray Nun said she was going even farther, that she was visiting the entire countryside to beg for the poor in her community's care.

"In that case," asked Maman, "would you be willing to take care of my little girl as far as Lourdes? Her aunt will come to meet her there."

29

The Gray Nun took good care of me. Searching through her pockets she found some candies, which must long have reposed there; they were blanketed in that kind of fine woolen fuzz that dwells in the depths of pockets. At one village, where we made a five-minute stop, she dashed off to buy me an ice-cream cone. I only hope that she did not spend alms collected for the poor to pay for it!

When I arrived at my aunt's house, it was suppertime. I at once sat down to eat, with my hat still on. My aunt had not yet received the bed she had borrowed for me in the village. I was given a choice between a small space in the big bed with my three cousins or a mattress all to myself on the floor. I took the mattress. First I removed my dress; then, at the last moment, before stretching out on the mattress, I removed my pink hat, which I placed on the floor close beside me, most likely with the notion of having it at hand the moment I woke up. My aunt, perhaps fearful that in getting up during the night some one might step on my hat, picked it up to place it on the bureau; but instead she perched it in the moonlight on a statue of Saint Anne which happened to stand there, and I began to moan quietly to myself.

It was not solely because my aunt had taken the hat away. Suddenly I had felt sad about being so far from home, at my aunt's, whom I did not know very well, and sleeping on a mattress on the floor into the bargain. Then she put my hat back beside me and said, "Silly girl."

The next day I went down to breakfast with my pink hat on my head, and the rest of me only half dressed. I asked my aunt to button my dress down the back . . . and I was quite happy for an hour or two. In my aunt's garden there was a tiny swing suspended between two spindly little trees. When I was up in the air, I could see far away, under the brim of my pink hat. I could even see, beyond a slight rise in the ground, near a slope on the road, a pretty house in the distance. On the porch were seated two old people who, like two cats, seemed to have nothing to do except warm themselves in the sun. I began to wish that I were in the house belonging to the two old people. In the end I convinced myself that I had known them a long while, that they were expecting me at their house. Often I told myself such tales, and I believed them.

When I was high enough in the sky, I was happy, but each time the swing sank back, I found myself in a minute garden, shut in on all sides. My three cousins were below me, at the foot of the small trees, sitting on kitchen chairs. They were little girls piously and strictly brought up; one was darning clothes with tiny, tiny stitches; another was knitting away at a huge black stocking; the third was reading a big book in a shrill, tedious voice. She had got as far as Saint Ignatius. The whining little voice followed me when I bounded back into the air. Up there I rediscovered the highway, the blue hills, and also the house of the two old people so snug on their doorstep. I thrust myself forward harder and harder to rise higher and higher. All this swinging finally made me sick at my stomach. Once off the swing, I looked everywhere for a way out of this puny garden. My aunt had fastened the gate with a stiff, heavy rope; my mother had probably warned her of my inclination to wander. I could not succeed in undoing the knot, nor could I wriggle under the fence.

During the afternoon the little old man came past my aunt's house. In his hand he held a sort of string bag; he must have been on his way to get provisions. He had a large beard. From behind the gate I politely greeted him, and he, laughing a bit, returned my wave with a wink. And he said, "You have a pretty little hat."

I was still there when he went by again, an hour later, his bag stuffed with packages. My aunt and my cousins were in the house doing chores or cutting out work for themselves; everyone in this tiresome family always had her task before her, and when that task was finished, the poor wretch went looking about for another. I called out softly to the bearded old man, putting a finger on my lips to urge his own silence. When he was very close, I asked him: "Monsieur, would you be kind enough to untie this big knot?"

Laughing a little, but soundlessly as I had requested him, he undid the knot. Then he went on, shuffling slowly, his hands at his back, thus dangling his bag behind him. The dirt road ahead seemed fine and long, mounting by short gray slopes. I began following the old man. He turned toward me. He took his pipe out of his mouth. He asked, "Wherever are you going?"

I ran the short distance between us and put my hand in his. I said to him, "With you."

We arrived together at his pretty house, wholly surrounded by flowers. When she saw me, the little old woman, sitting on one of the front steps, asked the old man, "Where did you pick her up?"

The old man smiled into his beard; he motioned with his head and shoulders to indicate some place behind us, but did not let go my hand. And the kindly old woman asked me, "Are you hungry?"

I nodded. Then the good soul pulled open a trap door and disappeared into the cellar to fetch some strawberry jam; she cut some slices of the whitest bread I ever saw; she gave me the best milk I ever tasted. What a lovely afternoon! I don't believe the old people asked me a single question. Certainly nothing so silly as, "Where did you come from? . . . What are you up to, hereabouts? . . ." We were very well pleased with each other, all three of us together on the porch, looking at each other and laughing soundlessly, just with our eyes and the corners of our lips.

Later on the villagers said that I had spent almost the whole day at the old people's house, that during all that time my aunt had almost lost her mind worrying; that first she had gone asking about me all over the village: "Have you seen a little pink hat going by?" Then they had even searched the wells. A very strange thing: to me it didn't seem long . . . not at all long.

Darkness was beginning to fall when suddenly I saw my aunt on the road, moving along at a brisk pace. In her hand she held a little stick, and she looked like someone who wanted to use it. The poor old people probably appeared more worried than I did. My aunt was scanning the whole countryside with her eyes; she did not yet know where I was; the bushes on that side of the road must have kept me from her sight; I might even have had time to hide more effectively. But when she raised her head, my aunt must have seen through the lilacs the crown of my pink hat. Her face immediately relaxed. Her eyes were no longer in the least angry. Her pace grew auspiciously slower. The stick fell from her hands.

And as for me, I ran out to meet my aunt and thrust my hand into hers.

## TO PREVENT A MARRIAGE

Mother and I were rolling along in a train toward Saskatchewan, on our way there to prevent a marriage.

I remember my father had come home one evening from one of his trips among the Dukhobors; he was deathly pale, upset, and nervous. He had said to Maman, "You have got to go out there, Eveline, and try to make her listen to reason. I've tried. But you know me; I must have been too violent. I didn't succeed in talking to her as I should have. You must go, Eveline, and prevent this marriage at all costs."

Then Maman had objected, "How about our youngest, Edouard?"

Since I had been born, Maman had not left me alone for a single day. And my father had replied, "Take her along. I have your pass. As for her, she is not yet old enough to have to pay a fare . . . or at most, half-fare!"

It was handy still to be too small to have to pay on the railroad. During those years I traveled a lot, but I was so young I remember little about it, save for this particular trip.

We had been in the train for quite some time. Maman

was seated facing me, her hands on her skirt, unaware of the passing countryside. She must have been going over in her mind what she would say to my big sister Georgianna. I had never seen much of Georgianna, who, the very year I was born, had gone to teach school in Saskatchewan. There was a photograph of her at home. Her hair was done up in two heavy black braids, tied with a ribbon above her ears, and in this picture she had excessively eloquent eyes. Even in a photograph, Georgianna looked as though she were ready to jump up and say, "Here I am! . . ." and then burst into laughter at everyone's surprise.

Propped against her plush seat, from time to time Maman assumed a look of wrath; she moved her lips as though framing a speech filled with reproaches. Then she must have recalled what my father had said: "Gentleness . . . be patient . . ." for she shifted to an imploring expression, truly most sorrowful. I was sad to see Maman talking to herself, inside herself, like that.

But most of the time I had my face glued to the window. It's odd: it seemed to me, it still seems to me, that the whole of this long trip must have taken place at night. Yet it is quite certain that at least a good part of it was by daylight. Moreover, I remember the burned-bread color of the land; at night I could not have seen it, nor that such, indeed, was the color of the grasses and of the soil itself. The country had been flat for a long, long while, then marked with an occasional low mound, then wholly flat again. There were small wooden houses around grain elevators painted dark red. I have always thought that the word "Estevan," which I can link to no exact recollection, must date from this trip; that perhaps I spelled it out on the front of some railroad station on the plains. I also read the big letters painted in black on the grain elevators:

"Manitoba Wheat Pool," and then it became "Saskatchewan Wheat Pool."

"Are we in Saskatchewan?" I asked Maman, and was about to feel pleased, because passing from one province to another seemed to me so great an adventure that it would certainly and completely transform Maman and me, perhaps make us happy.

Yet Maman, who certainly also loved adventure, only gave me a distracted nod, as though it was as sad in Saskatchewan as in Manitoba.

We got off the train, and this time it must really have been night, for of this big village I remember only the name, deciphered in the glow of an adventitious light, perhaps the locomotive's blazing eye. It was Shonovan.

There was a long wait for another train, which was to carry us over the last lap of our journey to Georgianna. We were sitting side by side in the almost dark waiting room. Maman had wrapped me in her coat and told me to sleep. But I couldn't. Cut off now from the occupation of reading the names on stations or the letters on the grain elevators, I felt seized by a sort of fear of this Saskatchewan – wholly dark and unknown – where we were stranded, so alone, upon a wooden bench. Often, thinking that I was asleep or in order to calm me, Maman brushed my cheek with her hand . . . and I felt her golden wedding ring scratch lightly over it.

But I was thinking hard. And abruptly I asked her: "So in real life it's wrong to get married?"

Then Maman told me that sometimes it was right, even very right.

"But why must Georgianna be prevented from marrying at all costs?"

"Because she is still too young," said Maman.

"You have to be old to get married?"

"Not too old, though," Maman replied.

And then she told me, "Don't worry your head about it. We may still succeed. Say a prayer that we do."

It was thoughtful of her to include me in the purpose of our trip. But I must have gone to sleep. And certainly Maman must have carried me in her arms to the second train and, later, to the house where Georgianna had her lodgings, for when I woke up I was lying in a bed, and in the next room I heard Maman and Georgianna talking heatedly.

I believe all this certainly transpired at night; I am almost sure it did . . . although the same dim glow hovers over this whole journey – I mean not darkness so much as an absence of real light – the same indefinite color penetrated by the noise of the rails, then by bursts of talk.

Maman must have forgotten what my father had so urgently recommended to her. I heard her say, "Don't talk so loud; you'll wake up your little sister," but she herself was raising her voice. "Georgianna, listen to me, listen to my experience. Your father says this boy is no good."

"That's not true," said Georgianna.

Then louder still Maman asked, "Why do you insist on creating your own unhappiness?"

And Georgianna kept repeating and repeating the same thing: "I love him; I'm going to get married. I love him. . . ."

Afterward, almost always throughout my life, I have been unable to hear a human being say, "I love . . ." without feeling my heart contract with fear, and wanting with both arms to clasp that so sadly vulnerable being and protect it.

I did not know Georgianna well enough to take her side against Maman. Yet it seemed to me someone ought to have supported her, because of the degree of pride in her voice when she reiterated, "I love him, you hear, I love him! No one will make me change my mind."

"Poor Georgianna," Maman then exclaimed, "you talk of love as though it would last. . . . But when it goes . . . if there is nothing to take its place . . . it's horrible!"

They must have been walking as they talked, perhaps moving toward each other, or – quite the opposite – drawing apart. On the walls of the room where I lay I could see their shadows move. A lamp projected their gestures before my eyes, and finally I could distinguish Maman's, which were despairing, from Georgianna's. From time to time Maman would raise her arms toward Heaven, like a person wholly disheartened.

I recall almost nothing, any longer, of the other day we must have spent at Georgianna's, almost nothing of that sojourn until the moment when we were again on a train and evidently had failed in our undertaking.

I saw in reverse – and looking completely different – all the same dark red little Saskatchewan villages, the wheat fields, the elevators with their big, black lettering.

But we did have an adventure.

Along the route we were taking, the Dukhobors had burned a bridge in protest against some governmental legislation. All that remained were the rails, barely supported by a few half-burned ties. The train could not risk a crossing. All the passengers were ordered off, with their baggage, and the plan was to carry us to the other side of the river, not more than five or six at a time, in a handcar. The adults were far from stronghearted; several cried out that we were going to die and became hysterical. But I was not afraid, and sat with my legs dangling over the water, held tight by my mother, who had her arm securely around my waist. A railroad man supplied the motive power for the small vehicle, which made good time. I thought it was fun. Never before had I crossed a river of which I could very clearly see the water through a bridge almost entirely burned away.

The travelers were furious with the Dukhobors. They should be thrown into jail, said one, and another asked why we received into our country people who would not conform to its laws. I was on the point of saying that my father was very fond of his Dukhobors, that he had settled them in Saskatchewan, and that he didn't think them wicked. Maman cut me short and told me to keep quiet; she said it was no time to proclaim to everyone that my father was friendly with his Dukhobors.

When we reached the other side of the river, the conductor himself came to tell us that help was on the way, not to be upset, the company would take good care of us and would get us to Regina; from there we could continue on a regular train.

On that side of the river there was a little knoll, and everyone sat down on it in the grass. It must have been afternoon. This was the only moment of the trip when I remember having seen the rays of the sun; they shone upon the knoll and on the faces, which eventually lost their angry looks. I was the only child among the travelers, and I was given so many oranges and so much candy that Maman begged the good people not to give me any more. Up on the hillock it was just like a big picnic; the grass was strewn with orange peels, nutshells, greasy papers, and people everywhere were singing – everyone was singing except Maman and I. Then I thought I would busy myself picking wild flowers to make myself a small bouquet, but Maman called me back again: that day she seemed not to want me to wander even a few steps away.

The rescue train arrived; it consisted merely of two boxcars, red like the grain elevators, and with no openings besides their heavy, sliding doors. The people were displeased; they complained, "Yes, the company is certainly taking good care of us; it's sending us off in boxcars!" Then all at once night fell; I think it comes quicker in Saskatchewan than anywhere else. A railroad employee was waving a lantern; it served the travelers as a guide through the darkness and helped them clamber into the cars, which naturally were not provided with steps. I was picked up in his arms and put inside like a bundle of goods. The country around us was pitch black; there were no farms in those parts; it was the real plain, without dwellings or lights. But along the railway there was movement; lanterns slid quickly up and down the right of way. English voices crisscrossed: "All right? . . . All right. . . . Ready? . . . All clear. . . ."

Then a lantern was hung from the ceiling of the boxcar. It gave little illumination, just enough to see the bare planks within which we were enclosed. Almost all the travelers sat on the floor; Maman and I were seated on our suitcase. Once again Maman had wrapped me in her coat. And soon we felt we were in motion, but just barely so; the track must have been damaged for a considerable distance. With the heavy doors slid shut upon us, it was like a dream in which you know you are moving forward a little, yet how do you know it?

Someone had a phonograph and records, and he played blues and jazz. Couples began to dance on the bit of free space between the two rows of people sitting on the floor. The light was faltering; the couples cast huge shadows which danced on the walls . . . shadows advancing, receding. Sometimes they came apart . . . then melted together again.

An old lady near Maman complained, "Isn't it dreadful? Young people who an hour ago did not know each other – and look at them, in each other's arms! Think of dancing at such a moment!"

Then they danced something even worse – a tango. I felt Maman stiffen beside me. My head was in the hollow of her shoulder. She put her hand on my eyes to induce me to close them, perhaps to prevent my seeing the dancers. But through her fingers I watched the shadows on the wall . . .

And I asked Maman: "Georgianna wouldn't listen to you? Will she be unhappy, as you said?"

Maman certainly hoped she wouldn't.

Then I asked her what was necessary for people to get married.

"They must love each other. . . ."

"But Georgianna says she's in love. . . ."

"She thinks she's in love," said Maman.

"And the Dukhobors . . . why do they burn down bridges?"

"They are visionaries," replied Maman; "they use bad means to accomplish what are most likely good ends."

"Don't you know it – for good and all – when you're in love?"

"Sometimes not," Maman answered.

"You knew it, though?"

"I thought I knew. . . ."

Then my mother became vexed. She seemed very put out with me. She said: "You're too prying! It's not your problem . . . all that. . . . Forget it. . . . Go to sleep. . . ."

## A BIT OF YELLOW RIBBON

My sister Odette was then like a princess among us. For a year she had done tatting – nothing but tatting; then she worked in raffia. The next year she practiced a prelude by Rachmaninoff; now her heart was attracted to the mystical life, and she faithfully attended the devotions of the month of Mary, "which is the loveliest," then those of the month of the Sacred Heart, and visited as well the little Massabielle Grotto which had been reproduced in our region; but since there was no single protruding bit of stone for twenty miles around, it had had to be dug in soft earth; at all seasons the grotto would cave in. When people pointed out to my mother that, with all the things she had to take care of, she might have expected more help from Odette, my mother would reply, "She does help me. . . . She prays for us."

For my part, in those days I thought Odette lucky beyond all belief. I recall the alpaca skirts she wore, almost as high as her ankles. You could see her handsome high shoes, the ends of which were pointed and turned up a bit, like the prow of a boat; a special hook was required for their ten little black buttons. She also wore vastly padded bodices with big sailor collars, made of so sheer a silk that she had to use corset covers underneath; but since these were equally thin, Odette had to wear yet another piece of clothing underneath them. The loveliest thing she possessed, though, in my opinion, was the outfit she wore to go motoring with her bosom friend Carmel, who was the daughter of wealthy parents. Odette would slip on a full raglan coat, beige in color – already she was beginning to have the look of an explorer – dark glasses, and a sort of helmet with a visor from which hung a full veil intended to protect her against the dust of the road. Thus clad she would sometimes go as far as ten miles away with Carmel in her automobile.

Perhaps I admired Odette too much really to love her. Then, too, several of the chores she imposed upon me were grievous to me. Using the excuse that I was small enough to slip under it easily, she would send me under the table to dust its heavy legs, which were elaborately ornamented with twists and curlicues, with scrolls and arabesques. And she, who could have no idea what was beneath that table, urged me to twist my dusting rag into a tiny, tiny point so as not to miss reaching the very bottoms of all the holes in the carving. She also made me dust the banister of our staircase, with its eighteen bars almost as tortured as the table legs – and then she would claim that I was soldiering at the job!

Above all, however, I was terribly envious of Odette's possessions. Her blue room, for instance, the nicest in the house! Maman said that Odette deserved it because she was twenty years old – I failed to see that this was any reason – and also because she was neat and orderly. Yes, she was orderly after a fashion, which consisted – probably the better to hide them from my eyes – in stuffing precious, mysterious little things into very small boxes, which she then placed in medium-sized boxes that were in turn enclosed in larger boxes still.

I was forbidden so much as to put a foot on the doorsill of Odette's room.

"You put one foot there one day," she would say, "and on the next the other foot is there, too!"

Despite everything, it once happened that as I was passing Odette's room I stopped two fingers' width from the sill and saw protruding from an ill-closed drawer a bit of yellow ribbon.

Instantly I longed for that yellow ribbon with so much intensity that I do not recall ever since having set my heart so much on any other object.

Yet why? To wind it around my doll's hair? Or around my own, which had gotten into a thorough tangle, perhaps in the hope that I might thus make myself more presentable? Or only to tie around the neck of my big gray cat which slept all day under the currant bushes? I no longer know; I can remember only my passion of desire for that bit of yellow ribbon.

I at once considered every tactical approach and elected one coinciding with an opinion of mother's, which held that "what you ask for very politely, with all your heart, you obtain." I went off to find Odette, all honey sweet: "Dear, kind, wonderful Dédette! . . ."

"What do you want now?" she asked, ruining all my softening strategy.

"Your lovely yellow ribbon, please, Odette . . ." I went on, but with a greatly diminished sweetness, perhaps already on a war footing.

I have never seen a person react so quickly as Odette,

jump so fast to false conclusions, search me with so penetrating a look, and accuse me so basely: "You nosy little brat! Miss Meddlesome! You've been going through my bureau drawers again!"

This dreadful reputation I don't think was merited, since I almost always stopped short at the edge of what was forbidden . . . but I had an imaginative eye, and did not an inch of ribbon hanging out of the corner of a drawer allow one to presume a great length of it inside?

In any case, I was so hurt that I retreated to the hut I then possessed in the far reaches of the garden – a hut constructed as though to stage theatricals, since, just like a stage, it had only three sides; I had run short of planks to close it in on all four.

Meanwhile, my mother was giving signs of those strange adult emotions that are neither wholly sorrow nor wholly joy. From time to time I noticed that her eyelids were reddened; then in Maman's beautiful brown eyes, even though they were swollen, I watched rise the sun of happiness, yet a happiness so difficult to reach, so unknown, that I was afraid of it.

I did not like seeing my mother distraught in this way; here was for me a beginning of insecurity. Often I went close to her, asking her what was the matter, and she replied "Nothing," but looked at me the while with an odd intensity, as though I were going to disappear from before her very eyes. Then, telling me to run along, she would say, "You're still too young."

But one day as she sat darning in the two-seated swing, my mother called to me and told me: "It is time that you, too, were told the great news. Your sister Odette," she added, "has chosen the better part. . . ."

That did not astonish me in the least. To me it was obvious enough that Odette, having always had the better part, could only continue along the same line.

Baffled at my calm acceptance of this news, Maman explained to me: "You understand: she has chosen God."

That puzzled me somewhat. Up until then it had seemed to me rather that God was the one Who chose . . . as, for instance, when during the course of a picnic, He did *not* send us a good, spanking shower.

Maman continued, "Odette is going to become a nun."

And then there burst upon me the obvious, the wonderful, the unbelievable advantage accruing to me from all this. "Odette," I inquired, "is going to leave us all her things?"

Astonished, perhaps, that I was so perceptive, that I should so quickly have glimpsed what a religious vocation is, Maman talked to me like an adult. "Odette is going to give up everything," said she. As she spoke, my mother let her eyes linger over our fine trees, warm in the sunshine, the flowers blooming in their beds. "She will give up, before her time, her share of the world, her youth, even her freedom!"

But I interpreted it otherwise: her little yellow ribbon; and it was hard for me to conceal my delight. Not that I thought it bad, or even out of place, but the emotions which were growing complicated around me at that juncture confused me and left me at a loss.

I began to hover around Dédette. One day when she was kneeling on the floor, busily extracting things from her trunk, which lay open in the middle of her room, I halted on the doorsill and watched her.

"It doesn't look as though you really want to go," I said to her.

Her smile at me was so friendly that I began to squirm in my dress. I wasn't overeager, because of my secret plans, that she be on good terms with me.

"You may come in," said Odette. "Come on in, Petite Misère!"

I was watching her out of the comer of my eye; she was absorbed in reading old letters; a few she tore up, others she left intact and tucked away in one of her famous boxes. I didn't understand what there could be about this occupation to make one so sad, so alone. But I put off to the morrow any talk about the yellow ribbon.

Odette had reached the stage of taking from her trunk her sheer shirtwaists, her ten-button shoes, in order to distribute them . . . and I even saw her pull out a lady's motoring outfit.

"Oh! You're not going to give that away!"

I had protested with such heat that Dédette sat back on her heels a moment and gave me a little smile.

"What purpose do you think it will serve me now?" And she did me the very great honor of consulting me on the choice of persons to whom she should give her possessions. I gave her my advice wholeheartedly.

"Give your automobile clothes to Agnès, whatever you do."

"But Agnès is still too small. She'd be lost in them."

"That makes no difference; give them to Agnès. You ask me whom you should give them to; I say give them to Agnès. . . ."

Yet all that scarcely furthered my own business. Right beside Odette, free to examine without let every box, to handle them a little, even to open them, how happy might I have been had the feelings between us not been so muddled!

The next day I again sought Odette out, this time firmly determined to work on my own behalf, to obtain my share – after all, the most insignificant – of the goods she was bounteously passing around. I found her as she was the day before, sitting on the floor, but her hands idle at her sides, her eyes far away. What on earth do grownups see when, staring thus fixedly, they look at nothing? I wondered.

At any rate I made a good start. Perfectly aware of what this meant to me, I said to my sister, "Don't go, Dédette. We'll keep you all the same."

Her nostrils quivered, her lips began to tremble; I was very much afraid that she was also going to begin to cry. But no. She almost furiously set about pulling everything that remained in it out of the bottom of her trunk. She tossed boxes helter-skelter around her, without even stopping any longer to look at what was in them. I kept the sharpest eye I could upon this shower of boxes; without giving too great an appearance of doing so, I was looking for a bit of yellow ribbon, for I had caught no further glimpse of it since my sister had begun going over her belongings. But now things flew too fast, and although she no longer seemed inclined to prevent my rummaging as much as I chose, I did not dare do it, precisely because of this unexpected forbearance. And also I was quite lost amidst all the thoughts pouring in on me. One of those which upset me the most was to know how Odette, if she were to give away all her clothes, was going to be able to leave the house.

Then she showed me in a drawer piles of rough, coarse clothing made of unbleached cotton.

"You're going to wear those things?"

She nodded and I gave her my frank opinion: "They're ugly and they're going to scratch you."

She drew me to her. No more than a kitten did I like to be squeezed, held in people's arms; but briefly I let Odette have her way. She, too, was suddenly looking at me with great curiosity, as though she had never properly seen me before that day. With her fingers she tried to untangle my hair. "You don't comb it very often," she reproached me.

It was an old reproach, but made in so affectionate a tone that it reawakened in me the troublesomeness, the memory of the sad things in my life, and Heaven only knows what other distasteful things, and I began to pull at my ear.

"Nor should you," Dédette told me, "pull your ear all the time."

So much perseverance in following her everywhere could have been interpreted as proof of an affection uncommon in a child of my age. Perhaps Odette reproached herself for not having entirely deserved it. I hesitated to destroy so strong an illusion and, at the same stroke, the picture of me as a dear and affectionate little sister which she was creating in her mind, and which did not wholly displease me. ·

With lowered head I moved away – and not a word concerning the yellow ribbon. . . . Yet the day of Odette's leaving was drawing ever closer!

I hadn't many more opportunities to catch her alone; now she was making the rounds of the relatives and friends. I regretted the loss of so many auspicious occasions, so many moments that had been favorable for stating my wish.

One day we had what was supposed to be a festive meal, at which everyone said there could be no greater happiness than that of giving a child to God; in spite of this our friends and relatives had trouble swallowing the good things set before them; the one time when we had so many rare dishes all at once, I found it sad that no one had any appetite.

Then, in two rented automobiles, we went to take Dédette and her friend Carmel to the station: the decision of one, my mother said, had carried the day with the other. Dédette's trunk had gone on ahead, and from time to time an anxious thought beset me: Might not my sister have renounced all save the yellow ribbon? In a small box, tied around a package of letters, it might be headed toward Montreal.

Under the high black ceiling, standing in a tight group, the relatives were weeping, especially Maman, who kept saying, "A child in religion is a guarantee of Heaven."

And then I, too, began to cry. I don't know exactly why. It seemed in those days I could cry at will, because it was appropriate, or to make others have a better opinion of me. But I think that from that very day onward, in order to cry I no longer needed to see others weep.

Odette had kissed each of us in turn. She had climbed onto the step of the car; I was there among the others, in my new dress, my hair neatly combed, right beside the train which was about to leave. And abruptly, very impulsively, Odette picked me off the ground and nearly hugged the breath out of me. She was saying, "Good-by, tousle-head! . . . Good-by! . . . Be a good girl! . . . Never be naughty! . . ."

Then, clinging to Odette like a kitten to a post, crying on her neck, I asked her: "Dédette! . . . Dédette! . . . Your little yellow ribbon . . . if you want to! . . ."

"Yes . . . yes . . . it's in your room," she said, putting me back on the platform, for the train was moving.

And it was for me, for me above all, I believe, that Odette so long – as long as she was in sight – waved her handkerchief.

After that, whatever became of the little yellow ribbon . . . I no longer remember.

## MY WHOOPING COUGH

Blessed be my whooping cough! I coughed, I turned blue in the face; I lost all taste for food; my lungs must at times have cried out for air, and, as Maman put it, I "sang like a rooster." She would then hold me close, stroke me with her hand. A cruel sickness it is, which cuts off a child's breath and makes him counterfeit a cock! At last, once my coughing fits ceased, I once more desired to go play with my little friends, and I cried because they would not let me. Truly this was the worst illnesses I had suffered, since it forbade my going near other children, and obliged me to fend them off if, in the goodness of their hearts and heedless of the disease, they insisted upon coming too close. Just as a leper tinkles his warning bell, I had to call out, "I have whooping cough; don't come near me!"

That was when Papa went to Winnipeg to buy me a hammock.

I spent almost all my time sitting in a tiny chair on the porch, wrapped up in woolens despite the heat, just like a little old lady, and wishing . . . wishing! Papa came home with a huge package under his arm. He undid it, and I saw the lovely hammock, woven in bright colors; red, blue, and – I think – yellow. My father installed it between two columns supporting our porch roof. Thus, said he, I should be partly in the sun and partly in the shade. Later Papa attached a rope to a tree not far from the porch; by pulling a little on this rope, I could swing without effort. My father showed me how: a slight pressure on the rope, and a slow, gentle swell would carry me along. Maman put a clean pillow in my hammock; and when I was stretched out in it, they all came to see whether I seemed comfortable there.

But that wasn't enough to make up for my whooping cough. From Winnipeg Papa had brought something else, which he unwrapped before my eyes. And then, although I was still so very weak, I laughed a little . . . with happiness. It was – do you remember them? I don't yet know their proper name; mine I called my "glass song" – an object made of thin strips of colored glass, loosely attached by their upper ends; and when they moved, gently striking each other at the least breath of air, they made a strange and charming tinkling sound. I had heard its fascinating music I know not where, perhaps in the home of some of our friends; probably the tiny chime had been placed above a door; anyway, ever since, I had longed for one with all my soul. Yes, my soul aspired to listen to this soft music for children, without complex notes, without the least melody, but which I remembered as whimsical, silvery, exotic, too; with it in your ears, unknown forests spread before you, forests of bamboo, perhaps, while natives slipped between the noded trees. Was it an expensive thing, hard to find? I had long begged for one; then, at the uselessness of my prayers, I had ceased speaking of it.

My eyes watched my father's every movement; he stood on a stepladder, attached the small glass chime to the porch

ceiling, just above me, so that as I lay in my hammock, I had
only to raise my glance to watch the thin slivers flutter. How
many hours, how many weeks did I spend seeking to understand how the delicate music was produced? Would that particular strip begin trembling? Would the red one give the purer
sound? What made the harmony? . . .

Was all this lost time? Then why is it that the time of
futile questions, of minute problems probed to no effect, is the
time that recurs and recurs to the soul as the time it has used
the best?

I must have spent the whole summer, almost all the
summer, in the depths of my hammock . . . and yet it comes
back to me as all one single warm and quiet moment, a
moment fixed in a tinkling of music as bright as the sun.

At first there were times, as I grew a trifle better, when
perhaps I wanted to leave the hammock and, hanging onto
each column in turn, work my way to the end of the porch.
This row of brilliant white columns, tacked on the front of our
otherwise very ordinary house, gave it what I recall as a certain
air of grandness; indeed, it was its only redeeming trait. Or is
it, rather, an enhancement created by my memory which
makes me see it today as a sort of Greek temple on our modest
Rue Deschambault? However that may be, from column to
column I dragged myself to see what games the children were
playing, how far they had progressed in erecting a tent village;
and I still worried a bit as to whether perhaps they missed me.

Then it seems to me that I drew far away from all such
things, that at a bound I outgrew what people call a stage in
one's life. All alone in my hammock, rocked only by the wind.
I discovered other play how vastly more rare and fascinating!
The wind's play, for instance. For here indeed was the musi-
cian! Had he as instrument only the telephone wires or the

branches of the trees or a few stalks of grass or the clothesline pulley, he produced upon them lovely sounds, sounds wholly distinguishable one from the other. It was on the telephone wires, I think, that he was at his most joyful; one could almost make out the sung words of a long conversation, rustling and vague, perhaps come along the wires from a distant city. During that interval I discovered almost all the things in nature I have never since ceased to hold dear: the motion of the leaves of a tree when you watch them from below, under their shelter; their nether sides, like the bellies of small animals, softer, paler, shyer than their faces. And basically all my life's voyages ever since have merely been going back to try to recapture what I had possessed in that hammock – and without seeking it.

Indeed, within myself, where I could plunge any time I wished, so close to me that I might never have perceived them – there were the pure marvels! Why does one not learn sooner that one is, oneself, one's best, one's dearest companion? Why this great fear of solitude, which is merely an intimate commerce with the sole true companion? Without him, would not the whole of life be a wilderness?

And why had no one told me that running, skipping rope, walking on stilts, climbing about in barns were merely vulgar games, soon stale and outworn? But to behold in the sky a white castle, see ride up toward it a knight mounted on a white horse, whose mane and legs come apart as he approaches . . . and now the horse is larger than the castle . . . then suddenly both castle and knight melt away in the sun. . . . Or then again, in the hammock as in some towering caravel, sailing into the waters of the south . . . and already you hear the island tom-toms; the queen is preparing to feed you tiny turtles and fruits; high into a palm tree a tiny naked Negro has clambered, now swinging in the wind like a feather. . . . Oh, such are games worth playing with all your heart!

But sometimes, too, I played at making myself sad. I pretended that we, everyone in the house, was dead; a crepe bow hung at our door, and people were saying the rosary around our coffins; sometimes I even flinched at a drop of the holy water being sprinkled on my lifeless face. Then I played at being revived; I sent home the friends and stricken relatives; I brought the dead back to life; in their honor I gave a banquet, and we ate nothing but blue plums.

I dozed from one dream to another; sometimes I carried into my unconscious dream the light, delicate web of the waking dreams, and in the same way the dream of ocean depths followed me when I wakened, and mingled with the fresh voyages I was to take. The swaying of my hammock helped the thread of my tales. Is it not curious? A slow, soft motion and the imagination is on its way! Docile, docile to the least impetus, a tiny swaying is all it needs. There is an anxiety, it would seem, which leaves us the moment we are in a motion that costs us no effort. Perhaps this surcease is known only to those who have learned how to rock gently to and fro!

Then occasionally the rope slipped from my outstretched hand. The wind grew still; a hot breath passed over me; it was as though I were in the Sargasso Sea, where sails fall slack. . . . During my whooping cough time, I effortlessly rediscovered what I had learned at school or read in books and thought forgotten – at least the things that had pleased me – the Cape of Good Hope, Drake, Elizabeth's Captain . . . Sir Walter Raleigh! . . . Very often only the names kept me company. There must have been some of them of whose meaning I could not possibly have known anything, which I probably loved for their sound alone, and which I kept repeating all summer; one of these names was *Eldorado*.

But at times the hammock no longer rocked me; my sails went limp; unconsciously, maybe, I whimpered at having come back to land.

Then someone, as he passed by me, gently gave a little shove to the hammock. Was he, then, aware that, like an opium eater in his trance, I was the slave of motion, and that a flat calm awakened me from my dream world? A hand gave the hammock a tiny push. Sometimes even a face leaned over mine buried in the hammock's deepest depths, and so hollow, so thin, so deeply hidden, said they, that only my eyes were there. But if the eyes were to close, then what would remain? They also said that I weighed no more at eight than formerly I had when I was four. Such retrogression terrified them. As for me, I found this backward movement an interesting business. Moving in reverse, would I not return to whence I came? I was free, so light, forever on my travels!

Yes, they often bent down over me. I kept my eyes closed, for I always knew who was looking at me – perhaps by the person's breathing – and by I know not what mysterious emanation of tenderness which finds no obstacle in closed eyelids. . . . It was Alicia, or Agnès, sometimes both together. . . . I did not open my eyes because what I had once beheld in those bent faces was too beautiful, was more than I could bear.

For – and did I not know it from the beginning? – the hammock in the wind, the glass music, the hand that pushed the hammock – had I even a right to survive all this happiness?

# THE TITANIC

A great ship had been lost at sea, and for a long time, for years even, people talked about it at night gatherings in our Manitoba homes. A mere nothing, perhaps no more than a sharp gust of wind, would bring it back to mind. The raging gale – so vicious that particular night – probably recalled the disaster to us more vividly than usual.

First of all, out on the porch, there was that sound of footsteps none of us recognized. Someone was knocking the snow off his boots and walking toward the kitchen door. That was where we sat of an evening when it was very cold; and at such times, rather than trying the front door, people came straight to the back of the house, the only illuminated part, and therefore the most attractive. Moreover – it must be admitted – when a lot of snow had fallen in a short time, we did not clear off the whole porch; we did the easiest thing; we made a single path leading directly to the kitchen. The sound of the footsteps, then, by the time we were able to hear it over the wind, was already very close. Maman was visibly startled. She said, as though this night could bring forth nothing except danger, "Lord, what can that be!"

When the door opened, we beheld, surrounded by flurries of snow, a man wholly swathed in fur, his raccoon cap pushed down to his eyes, the collar of his greatcoat turned up; what little of his face we could see was red with cold, yet laughing; the eyes shone, the small mustache was stiff with frost.

"For Heaven's sake! . . . Majorique!" cried Maman, recognizing her youngest brother, who had come from the country to attend to some business in town. "Come in! What weather for you to be making us a visit! Do come in, come in quickly and warm yourself!"

Then she remembered to introduce him, for that evening we had with us a Monsieur Elie and his wife, Clémentine, both from the village of Lasalle, and when they came to town, they also, it seems to me, would end up at our home. Thereupon, even though we had several times in the last hour opened the door just to check on the strength of the gale, Maman asked about the weather. After all, during a Manitoba winter, was there any subject more fascinating to us than the current weather – at once our most mysterious and our most palpable enemy?

"Awful! Raging like a wild beast!" said my uncle Majorique.

Once he had slipped off his coat, he looked young, slight, and delighted to be alive, the part in his thick black hair cutting as deep as a path through meadow grass. "It wouldn't be much fun to be out at sea tonight," said he to Maman. Far-fetched remarks and comments in this vein he seemed to prefer to address to her.

For why was it that our own glacial plains, our poor frozen plains, did not suffice to give us an adequate idea of solitude, that to deal with the subject properly, we, people buried in the very depths of continental land, had to conjure up the ocean? Was it because we were specially gifted with

imagination and a fellow feeling for others who suffered? . . .
Monsieur Elie, stooping a bit in the shadow, spoke our
thoughts for us: "It must have been on a night like this that
the *Titanic* perished."

His wife almost never expressed an opinion in her
husband's presence; tonight, however, it was as though she did
have some will of her own: "Wasn't it rather on a foggy night
that that fine ship was lost, lock, stock, and barrel?"

I noticed that she said "Lock, stock, and barrel" just as
you might say "body and soul" about a man, but I wondered
what fog was.

One of them replied that it is like cotton wool pervad-
ing the whole atmosphere; another described it as a very thin
steam, like that exhaled by our kettle on the stove, but thicker
than that, of course, and cold into the bargain. My uncle told
me of a current of warm water which was loath to mingle with
the nearby icy water, and so the two struggled together. . . .
Was it, then, their breathing that prevented you from seeing?
I became aware how difficult it is to describe real things.
Maman, however, said that fog is a little like what happens in
our unhappy dreams, when a sixth sense warns us of a danger
we can neither touch nor see; it lies in wait in dead-white in-
visibility. . . . And then I had a fairly clear idea of the great
ship's torment, not far off Newfoundland.

"The sturdiest ship ever built!" exclaimed Monsieur Elie.
"None the less it hastened to its downfall, for God always
punishes pride."

In our kitchen, right about mother's sewing machine,
you could indeed look at God – God the Father, I mean. In
the picture's lower portion was depicted the Holy Family;
Jesus was young; Mary and Joseph were sitting there; they
seemed to be people like ourselves, happy all three to be

together; and occasionally I thought that the warmth from our big stove rejoiced them, too. But God the Father held Himself aloof in a Cloud. Was it His frowning brows that gave Him that look of always wanting to catch us in some wrongdoing?

"They were dancing," Monsieur Elie continued, "on board the ship. Dancing," he marveled, "in mid-ocean!"

"Do they have music to dance to on a boat?"

My uncle Majorique smiled a little at my question, but not to make fun of me. Quite the opposite; my uncle Majorique liked to explain things, and he was good at it, for he had at home a complete set of the Encyclopaedia Britannica. And on Manitoba farms in winter there remains little work to do; so my uncle would learn from his volumes how the telephone worked, or the principles of wireless telegraphy and radio. When he came to see us, he explained these things to us, with the help of very astute comparisons, and he would make diagrams that we might understand more clearly. So he began telling me about ocean liners: they were equipped with kitchens, pots and pans, libraries, parlors with chandeliers, fresh flowers, games of all sorts for the passengers' recreation, counters at which to settle bills, a small shipboard newspaper, a barber, a masseur, stewards; in short here was a town venturing forth upon the seas. . . . At night it was alive with lights that spilled out over the waves, and there were moments, maybe, when the black water seemed gladdened by them.

And – I know not why – as he kept listing what there was on board the ship, my heart was ill at ease, though I was eager to learn more. When my uncle added that certain completely up-to-date ships even boasted swimming pools, I got a picture at once curious and funny, but one that certainly did not make me laugh; on the contrary, I felt an unknown and terrifying sadness at the thought of people plunging into the water of a swimming pool contained within a vessel itself afloat upon infinite water. My uncle Majorique was answering Monsieur Elie: "True enough, they were dancing, but we must not forget the couples aboard the *Titanic* were almost all newlyweds, Monsieur . . . on their honeymoons! . . ."

Then Uncle Majorique saw the question in my eyes; he told me what a honeymoon is: "The time of love, at the beginning of a marriage, when all is beautiful. . . ."

"Later on does it become less beautiful?"

Everyone laughed a bit, but sheepishly, and exchanged glances that were none too open. Monsieur Elie seemed annoyed and in ill humor. Only my uncle Majorique did not appreciably change expression. And he told me that it was the time when married people could scarcely do without each other; when they were forever kissing and making much of one another. . . .

Maman then made Uncle Majorique a sign. He hummed a snatch of song. I was thinking of those poor people so happy to be together on the ship. Abruptly Monsieur Elie began to scold. He said of them, the folk on the *Titanic*, "Hammerstein! . . . Vanderbilt! . . . Big bankers from New York! . . . Those were the people on the *Titanic!* Millionaires!"

So in fact those poor people were rich!

"Yes," my uncle Majorique agreed, "wealthy couples, handsome, young, happy! . . ."

"And they thought their boat proof against all danger," said Monsieur Elie.

"Is there something wrong," I asked them, "about building a sturdy ship?"

Even Monsieur Elie seemed taken aback at my question. He granted that there was nothing wrong about it, probably nothing at all, but it most certainly was wrong to imagine oneself out of the reach of God's wrath. Yet why did he seem so pleased about God's wrath?

"Alas," said my uncle, "the captain had been warned of the presence of icebergs in the neighborhood. They might still have been saved had only the captain given orders to reduce the vessel's speed. But no; the *Titanic* was cutting through the waves at its normal speed – very fast for those days. . . ."

"An iceberg?" I asked. "What's that?" and I was afraid of the answer.

My uncle Majorique told me how mountains of ice break off from the Labrador ice masses; how unfortunate, even how cruel is our country, since these mountains drift down into the navigation routes . . . and under water they are seven or eight times larger than what appears on the surface.

So then I had a vivid picture of the graceful, sturdy white ship. With all its portholes brightly aglow, it slipped along our kitchen wall. Then, from Monsieur Elie's side, there moved straight toward the ship the monstrous mountain that had severed itself from Labrador. And they would meet at a point where the sea was at its worst. . . . Was there no way to warn them once again? . . . For surely the ocean is a vast expanse! . . .

"The *Titanic*'s foghorn," said my uncle, "resounded in this opaque silence . . . and then the time came when the echo that returned to the boat was close . . . very close. . . ."

We had half closed our eyes.

"The spur of ice," my uncle said, "had pierced the *Titanic* to its heart."

In a very low tone, as was usual with her when sorrow beset us, Maman asked, "Majorique, do you recall how much time elapsed between the moment of collision and the *Titanic*'s final disappearance?"

"Not much . . . maybe twenty minutes . . ."

I looked at the clock, watching its hands.

"Was it not then," Maman inquired, "that they began to sing 'Nearer My God to Thee'?"

The minutes were speeding by; I asked, "How does a boat go under?"

Monsieur Elie was pleased to enlighten me. "A sinking boat," said he, "slopes and slopes until it is almost upright in the water." He used his fountain pen to show me how and held it, point down, suspended over nothingness. "Then – suddenly – it plunges into the depths of the ocean. It is engulfed forever. Nothing, perhaps, disappears as completely as a ship sunk in the depths of the ocean. . . ."

"But the people," I cried, "what happened to the happy people, the Vanderbilts?"

"They had gotten the women and children into lifeboats," said my uncle, "but a number of these upset; the poor wretches thrashed around for a while in the icy water. . . ."

"But the children? Did the children, too, plunge down into the depths?"

"We should talk about other things," Maman said, after having glanced at me. "It's late . . . you should have been in bed long ago . . ."

I acted deaf. When stories were dreadful, and very interesting, sometimes Maman forgot to carry through with her orders.

"From some distance away a freighter could have come to their rescue," remarked my uncle, "but the wireless operator on the freighter, after receiving from the *Titanic* a message saying 'No cause for alarm,' laid aside his earphones. And so the *Titanic*'s SOS wandered about in the darkness, without at first finding a single listener. . . ."

"Yes," said Monsieur Elie, "from time to time God punishes human presumption in terrible ways."

"All the same," my uncle pointed out, "that has not stood in the way of building even larger and sturdier ships since then . . . and men are constantly getting more skillful at flying through the air. Who knows? . . . Tomorrow perhaps men will journey to the moon . . . or as far as the planet Mars. . . ."

"Lord in Heaven," sighed poor Clémentine Elie, "I'd rather die than see such things happen!"

"Perhaps it's inhabited," argued my uncle Majorique.

I crept over close beside him. He lifted me to his knees. He stroked my hair. "As for me," he said, "I'd like to live a long while; I'm curious to see what men will attempt."

God the Father, though, was in the clouds. Would airplanes climb as high as that? Would God let them by? . . . Would He want man to go as far as Mars? . . . Everywhere, within us, around us, it seemed to me we were plunged in fog.

# THE GADABOUTS

Toward the middle of the Provencher Bridge, Maman and I found ourselves surrounded by sea gulls; they flew low over the Red River. Maman took my hand and clasped it tight, as though to convey to me a movement of her soul. A hundred times a day Maman got a lift of joy from the world around us; sometimes it was nothing more than the wind or the flight of a bird that delighted her. Leaning on the parapet we watched the gulls for a long while. And all of a sudden, on that bridge, Maman told me that she would like to be able to go whenever and wherever she might choose. Maman told me she still longed to be free; she told me that what died last in the human heart must be the liking for freedom; that even suffering and misfortune did not wear thin within her this inclination toward liberty. . . . Maman quite frequently spoke to me of such notions, perhaps because I was too young to see anything wrong in them, perhaps also because she had no one else to whom she could speak of them.

Yet in the past Maman had already spoken of being free, and the only outcome had been even more children, much more sewing, much more work. As tied down as she was, why indeed did Maman never cease to wish for freedom?

As she watched the gulls, she began to smile, and she said to me, "One never knows! So many things happen! . . . Before I get really old, perhaps I'll travel, live through some adventure. . . ."

"You're already old," I told Maman.

"Not that old," Maman replied, a little put out. "You'll see yourself, when you're forty-nine; you'll believe you still have a few good years ahead of you."

"Oh!" I protested, "I'll never be forty-nine!"

And Maman agreed that she was rather old, that it was late true enough, to obtain from life all that she had wanted from it.

But what was it she had so much wanted from life? I had asked her. Was it not a house, her husband, I and the other children?

Maman said no; that, at least during her earliest youth, those were not the only things she had wanted; though – she added – her husband, her house, and her children she would not exchange for anything in the world.

We continued on our way toward Winnipeg's large stores, where, at the beginning of each month, we went to spend Papa's money; and almost all of it, alas, went for mere nothings, for things we could not do without. But the gulls accompanied our thoughts . . . as far as Eaton's . . . to the yard goods department. Maman had paused to look at a piece of navy-blue cloth. She unrolled a length of it which she held against herself from shoulder to hips; and standing in front of a mirror, Maman studied the reflection of the material along-side her face. She asked me what I thought.

"Wouldn't that make a fine suit for a trip?" she asked.

But I was annoyed that Maman could want for anything except being eternally chained to me and the house, and I displayed little enthusiasm; all the same her features next to the new cloth seemed to me a trifle less tired – but maybe it was Maman's smile, her timid yearning, which changed her whole appearance.

That time we did not buy the cloth; perhaps it was the following month . . . I'm not quite sure any longer. We went back to the yard goods counter, and now there wasn't much left of the material Maman had liked so much. The saleswoman assured us that within a week there would certainly be none. So Maman had a good quantity cut off, the bolt; carefully she supervised the clerk while the woman measured the required amount. Then my mother carried the bundle off under her arm, and we set out on foot; we had two miles to go, and I was tired of walking. But Maman, with her package close beside her, moved along briskly. Almost never had I seen her buy something for herself alone, and I couldn't get over my surprise. I was none too overjoyed to see this change in her, to see her think of her own tastes, indulge a whim; and yet I cannot say that I was displeased to see her walking without fatigue, her head held high, smiling to herself. Probably I wanted to hold captive those I loved, but I wanted them happy in their captivity.

I asked to take the tram, but Maman explained to me that we had spent a crazy sum of money and that now we should have to make up for it by pinching pennies. We recrossed the bridge, and the sea gulls greeted us with their little cry – so sharp, so strange! What good will it do Maman, I asked myself, to have a traveling suit? Certainly neither I nor my father nor the other children will ever let her go!

Papa was away. Often he was absent for a whole month or more. Papa was a highly considered man, an honored one;

yet it could not be denied that the house was much gayer when my father was not there. Papa could not endure having the least debt hanging over him; his first concern was to pay debts off, before anything else, and so much so that he rarely had time to be concerned over anything else. He also insisted that we tell him the precise truth, and nothing at times is more misleading than a precise truth; he did not like noise, and he wanted meals served on time, order in the house, the same things – always the same things – at the same hours, day after day.

Maman began to sew. The "in-between" girls came to see what she was making; when they saw that Maman was sewing for herself, they lost interest and trotted off, one to swing outdoors in the hammock, the other to read in her room. I alone remained near Maman, worried over what harm the freedom stirring in her heart might bring us.

Maman made her suit in two pieces: a skirt rather tight at the bottom, and a long jacket with two large accordion pockets, adorned with tabs of the same material, and on each tab there was a button; in addition, Maman added a "half-cape," as she called it, which hung down her back as far as the elbows.

When the suit was all basted together, Maman tried it on and asked me whether I thought it made her look like a traveler.

I said yes, that Maman looked just like a coachman. Whirling in front of me, she made the cape billow out as though the wind were in it. She looked so free that I couldn't restrain myself from pouting a bit.

Then, out of the trimmings that remained, by dint of piecing them together yet following the weave of the cloth, Maman succeeded in making me, too, a traveling jacket, exactly like hers, with accordion pockets, a very high, stiff little collar, the cape, and everything else. For the skirt we had to go back to Eaton's; by very good luck some of the cloth remained, but so little Maman got it at a reduction. From that moment on, I was no longer inimical to freedom.

Once our two suits were finished, Maman said to me, "I have an idea; let's go show ourselves to Mrs. O'Neill, as though we were all ready to leave. I have an idea she'll be tempted. Let's put on our dress jackets and walk by Mrs. O'Neill's just as though we were going a lot farther. . . ."

Mrs. O'Neill had come straight from Ireland to live in a house on Rue Desmeurons, two minutes away from ours, and she was bored to death, spending her time in her parlor gazing at etchings and engravings that depicted hazy landscapes, pale lakes, meadows so wet that when you looked at them you felt as though you wanted to sneeze. To someone come from such a country, our small city of wooden houses and sidewalks must have seemed very dry and dull. There were even moments when my mother, who had spent almost all her life there, found it tedious. Indeed, all the adults I knew in those days seemed to be bored. As for me, I was not bored. Probably I still possessed something I didn't know I had, but which, once you have lost it, you try all your life to rediscover!

Maman must have been a good judge of character. Mrs. O'Neill, who was sitting on her porch that day, the moment she saw us coming jumped up from her chair; she opened the screen door and came a few steps to meet us.

"My gracious! What lovely costumes you have! How well they'd suit me and my little Elizabeth!"

"They're not so much," said Maman; "I made them myself."

"How clever you are," said Mrs. O'Neill. "Oh dear! Turn around a little," she asked me, "so that I may see how that charming little cape is made. . . . It puts me in mind of my uncle Pat and the macfarlane he would wear to go to town. . . . Couldn't you make two other suits, just like them?" she asked Maman. "One for me and one for my little girl? And I'd also like those big pockets . . . you can put so much in them! . . ."

Maman then explained that the design was by way of being a creation, in short, an idea completely out of her own head, and that, generally speaking, one does not repeat creations.

"Oh! I'll gladly pay you whatever is necessary," said Mrs. O'Neill. "Oh, please!"

Maman had a few qualms of remorse at having accepted Mrs. O'Neill's order. "Perhaps it was not right of me to have done that," she said; "the Lord alone knows what I may have put in Mrs. O'Neill's head. It's unlikely that the suit, even when she has it for her own, can carry her back home to Ireland. Yet, on the other hand," Maman added, "I'll have fifty dollars from Mrs. O'Neill for the two creations and for the dresses I shall mend for her. So I'll not be using your father's money for the trip I'm going to take."

And she explained to me: "If God affords me the means to make enough money to leave, it's because He wants me to go."

God must have favoured my mother's ideas, for at the same juncture she received ten dollars from her brother Majorique.

At night, when all her other tasks were done, Maman made Mrs. O'Neill's and Elizabeth's suits; she made them of bottle green with black braid on the cuffs and collars, so that they were creations in themselves, perhaps even prettier than our own. In that way, said Maman, she was repairing the injury she had perchance done Mrs. O'Neill.

"Then, too," said Maman, "it's almost impossible, when one repeats the same piece of work, not to do a little better each time."

Maman's eyes were inflamed from having sewn so much at night. I realized that the desire for freedom ruled her almost as harshly as the duties of her condition in life.

Papa suspected nothing. He returned from Saskatchewan worn out and almost disheartened. His Dukhobors had stripped themselves naked and in that state had wandered all over their village, because the government wanted to force them to live like everyone else; and the Dukhobors had replied that God created us without a stitch of clothing. My father seemed weary of the human race, and he looked upon us with a trace of envy.

I remember that day we were all in the large, sunny kitchen, and each of us seemed busy at what pleased her – Maman sewing, Alicia embroidering; a saucepan was jiggling slightly on the stove; I was playing with the cat. And Papa said, "I don't know if all of you realize how lucky you are! A good roof over your heads; enough to eat; peace and tranquility. I wonder whether you appreciate your good fortune."

Maman looked a bit defiant. "Certainly," said she, "we appreciate what we have; yet all the same, from time to time, it would be nice to get away from the house."

She went on to explain. "There are times, Edouard, when I'd trade my life for yours: to travel, see new things, wander over the country. . . ."

As she talked, she became carried away; her eyes began to glow. I saw nothing in this so greatly to annoy Papa, but now he began to berate mother as a gadabout, a gypsy, an unstable person.

A little offended, Maman replied that it was all very well for a man to talk that way; that a man, because he had the luck to get out of the house, imagined that the house was a sort of paradise. . . .

Then Papa really lost his temper; he accused all Maman's family, saying they were a race of gadabouts, people who had never been able to settle down in one place. Whereupon Maman retorted that in all families there were tales to be told; that perhaps it was a good thing we did not know Papa's people, because among them, too, there were certainly faults to be found.

And Papa said, "Truth to tell, you ought to have been born in a gypsy caravan."

"You know, Edouard, that wouldn't have displeased me a bit!" Maman replied.

Then immediately she changed the subject. She became sweet and gentle. "Come eat, Edouard," said she. "I've made you a fine cabbage soup."

That day the meal included all Papa's favorite dishes. Later on, when Maman saw that Papa was serene once more, she launched a flanking attack: "You may rest assured, Edouard, that I shall never ask you for money to take a trip . . . you who are so thrifty and work so hard! . . . But if you could get me free passage . . ."

Papa must have been less restored to good temper than she had thought. He exploded at once. "Never," said Papa, "never shall I ask the government for any favors so that you may take a pleasure trip. . . . If there had been a death in the family . . ."

"Still, one doesn't travel merely to look at corpses," Maman complained. "Madame Guilbert had a pass to go see her relatives in the Province of Quebec. . . . I don't see why . . ."

"No," said my father, "I shan't have you go off on a jaunt at the country's expense."

"If you think that will impoverish the country . . ." Maman said, and she made Papa a prediction: "Do you want me to tell you something, Edouard? We shall always be poor; you will always be poor; you are too honest!"

They discussed the subject a while longer, but it was useless. Papa did not understand Maman . . . and perhaps Maman did not adequately understand that Papa, leading a wandering life, needed to find at home a stable, firm base, unchanging from year to year – if both of them were to be given full justice.

Papa once again departed for Saskatchewan to try to make his Dukhobors see the light. Seemingly he was making progress – by means of gentleness and patience. The Royal Police had got nowhere with prison. Later on I learned that in the new settlements Papa was altogether a different man from what he was at home, very understanding with his poor Slavs. Off there he was frequently jolly even; in a tent on the prairies, with his people, Papa was forever humming a tune. He traveled a great deal in a wagonette harnessed to a gray mare, and the tall grasses on either side of him must have billowed, while the partridges flushed from their small swamps. How sad! For had Papa behaved with us as he did with strangers, and Maman with him as she did when he was away, would they not have been perfectly happy together? . . .

Papa returned to his post, and the sea gulls returned to fly through our dreams and our thoughts.

II

But in order to break away, Maman had so many bonds to
sever that she became upset over it. I then perceived that freedom, too, grants the human heart small repose. Maman had
to part with Gervais, whom she sent to boarding school. At
the convent she asked to see Sister Edouard in the parlor. This
was our Odette, who now bore a new name. Maman asked her
to pray for a project about which she could tell her little, but
which was close to her heart. A risky project, said she; God
would perhaps view it askance. But Odette promised to pray
in any case.

Then the middle girls had to be disposed of. We took
them to Saint Anne-des-Chênes; the sisters at this convent
had made Maman a very reasonable price for the two of them
together – Alicia and Agnès. Both of them had handsome long
hair; in those days it took Maman a good hour each morning
to comb, brush, and braid their tresses. For a woman who
valued freedom, what chains she had forged herself! The two
middle girls also had dresses covered with flounces, made with
small, tight pleats and wide starched collars; to wash and iron
those dresses meant a good day's work for Maman.

The Sister Superior of this Saint Anne-des-Chênes
convent at once declared that in her institution they did not
permit complicated dresses or long, cumbersome hair.

Maman promised that Alicia would help her sister braid
her hair, and that Agnès would then help Alicia.

"Between two strokes of the bell!" said the Superior. "It's
obvious that you are not acquainted with life in a convent!"
She served Maman with an ultimatum: "Cut your girls' hair
or take them back home."

"You are harsh." said Maman; "it's as bad as though they
were taking the veil."

She asked that scissors be brought, and then some newspaper, which she spread on the convent's varnished hardwood floor. But just as she thrust the scissors into Alicia's hair, Maman said, "No, I can't do it . . . let's go back home together. . . ." All Maman's other daughters were blonde, their hair at least light brown. But Alicia's was extraordinarily fine, and "of the loveliest jet black," as my mother described it.

Meanwhile, Alicia and Agnès began to beg Maman to go ahead; they had long wanted to be like boys and freed of their heavy locks.

Then, her eyes closed, Maman gave the first clip with the shears. In the course of doing the job, she must have said to herself, "If I'm to spare my girls work, I might as well be thorough about it . . ." for she practically removed all the hair they possessed. When she saw their shorn locks, she began to lament: "Lord, whatever have I done! This is something your father will never forgive me."

I never saw a sadder house than ours when Maman and I got back to it. That it was so large had never struck us before, nor that it echoed the sound of one's voice from room to room. We began walking round on tiptoe.

"Noise certainly echoes in this house," said Maman; and she sat down to write Papa a letter.

"Dear Edouard," she wrote, "I'm leaving with the money I earned, but unfortunately I haven't enough to pay the tradespeople. . . ."

Over Maman's shoulder I read a good part of this letter, and I don't like to remember it. This was the first time in my life, I think, when I no longer wanted to be a grownup: to be a grownup involved giving too many explanations. "You will say, Edouard," Maman wrote, "that I ought to have asked your permission. But it's not certain that you would have given it . . . whereas now I leave with at least the benefit of the doubt. . . ."

Afterward we bolted the door of our house: we slipped the key under the mat and we went to the corner to wait for our tram in a cold, thin drizzle.

At the station, Maman already looked less guilty. For the trip we brought our own food along. If we were silly to go at all, we at least had to be sensible in other matters, especially in our small expenses.

### III

I found Canada immense, and it seemed that we had only crossed about a third of it. Maman likewise seemed proud that Canada should be so large a country. She confided to me that when you came down to it, and had circumstances permitted, she could have spent her life looking at people and cities; that she would have ended up a true nomad, and that that would have been her real misfortune. And I became aware how much travel made my mother seem younger; her eyes filled with sparks that glowed at the sight of almost everything we saw. The little evergreens, the water, the rocky ledges along the right of way – Maman beheld them all with love. "The world is fascinating," she would say. And I held it a little against Papa that he did not more often allow Maman to seem youthful. It's really a lovely thing to see an elderly woman take on once again the looks of a young girl. I knew that if I had been a husband, that's what I should best have liked to watch.

One entire day we skirted Lake Superior.

"It's the biggest lake in the world?"

Maman told me yes, she thought it was the world's biggest lake.

And I was proud that we people in Canada should own the biggest lake in the world.

"Is it bigger than Ontario?"

Maman laughed heartily. "How do you think it could be bigger than Ontario, since it is contained in Ontario?"

Ever since that day I have loved the word "Canada." Before, I had especially liked the "Pampas" or "Tierra del Fuego." From then on I was just as fond of "Canada." You can immediately sense that it is the name of a very large country. And even in those days, I think I should not have wished to live in one of those tiny little countries which are no more than a spot on the map of the world.

We spent yet another night on the train. The next day my mother became a little anxious, and when we entered the Windsor station, she frankly looked upset. It was because we had no one very close to us in Montreal. Maman had often claimed to have a lot of relatives there and, among others a certain Dr. Nault, her cousin, whose affectionate disposition could not have changed over the years. But in the station Maman told me that, after all, thirty-five years had elapsed since last she had seen this cousin Nault, that he had become wealthy, and that, when they became rich, people found it difficult to recall the things or the faces of other days.

We left our largest bag at the check room. We then found Dr. Nault's address in the phone book. We asked a dozen people what streetcar to take, and finally someone gave us the correct information. So we started off toward our cousin's home, taking with us our small valise only. "That way," Maman explained, "we shall not look like people who have come looking for an invitation to stay. Yet if our cousins insist on keeping us, at least we'll have what we need for the night."

And Maman must have begun to envision within herself the warm welcome we should receive, for I saw her smile inwardly, as though she were sure of Providence. There were times, though, when she preferred to call it "her star."

As for me, I must have taken more after my father than I had up till then believed. I began to worry about the adventures in which Maman might involve me. Night was falling. At heart I was afraid of Canada's metropolis. For that Montreal is a big place no one can deny.

Dr. Nault lived on Rachel Street. We walked along encountering no one save Jews, and then we entered an old-fashioned-looking pharmacy; the counters were full of big glass jars containing dried herbs and powders, on which were inscribed *Arsenic, Senna, Belladonna.* . . . I was in the process of reading all these words when I heard something stir behind a high counter. There stood a slight man, clad in black, with a black beard, very black eyes, and his head covered by a skullcap. Maman having asked him "Are you Doctor Nault?" the old chap replied, "Himself, in person."

"In that case, do you recognize me?" Maman asked, planting herself in front of the old fellow, her head cocked to one side and her lovely eyebrows arched, as she did when she looked in a mirror or wanted to be seen to best advantage.

Without hesitation the old man replied, "Not at all. Am I supposed to know you?"

At that moment a bell jangled on the other side of a partition, not far away. Dr. Nault removed his skullcap and said to us, "Forgive me: a medical customer . . ."

He opened a small door in the wall, which led from the

pharmacy into what looked to us like a doctor's office. We saw a woman patient, who was indeed entering this consulting room, but by a door that opened directly on the street.

Ten minutes passed. We saw the patient go out as she had entered, holding in her hand a slip of paper on which she seemed to be looking for an address, for she raised her eyes from the paper to the street number on the house. Arriving at the next door, which led into the pharmacy, she walked in. At the same instant Dr. Nault emerged through the small door in the wall; he put his skullcap back on his head. He was at his post as pharmacist when his patient walked up to the counter, and he took from her hands the paper he had given her in the consultation room. Maman and I of course realized that it was his own prescription which Dr. Nault, now the apothecary once more, was about to fill. And, indeed, he studiously read all that was written there and then proceeded to mix and grind together pinches of powders which he extracted from left and right, from lower and upper shelves, from almost all the glass jars. Maman made a gesture to silence my laughter. When his patient had taken her packet and had paid him, Dr. Nault turned to us, eager with curiosity.

"Samuel," Maman then asked him, "don't you remember the dozen broken eggs?"

The old fellow looked startled and put on his glasses the better to examine us. "Who are you, anyway?"

"Yes, indeed," said Maman, who, it seemed to me, did nothing to leave him guessing, "I am your cousin Eveline."

"Oh!" said the old man. "Where on earth have you dropped from?"

"From Manitoba," said Maman.

"Yes," he observed, "I did hear you'd gone into exile there. But what are you doing here? Didn't you get married?"

"I certainly am married,'" Maman replied; "this is my little daughter."

The old chap gave me a brief glance and began to ask questions anew: "But what in the world are you two doing hereabouts? Manitoba's not exactly around the corner! . . . "

"It certainly isn't,'" responded Maman, "but with modern means of transport – I mean the railroad – one can move about so quickly nowadays. . . . Have you any children, Samuel?"

"Eleven," said he. "But how on earth . . ."

"I was going through the neighborhood," said Maman; "I remembered little Samuel, who was always such a joker . . . Do you still play jokes, Samuel? And I thought I'd get some news of how things are going with you, about your family."

"I never thought I'd see you again," said the old fellow.

He made a motion, cast a vague glance at the ceiling. "You're not going to leave," said he, "without going upstairs. We live above. Let's go up," he added, without much warmth and scratching his head beneath his skull-cap.

On the stairs Maman whispered to me not to look so worried; if the Naults did not invite us, she would find other relatives; she had other strings to her bow.

We were seated on hard sofas facing Madame Nault, who was flanked right and left by her daughters. They all had their hands crossed over their skirts in precisely the same fashion, and all these women were clothed in unrelieved black. By way of politeness Maman inquired whether the family were in mourning, and Madame Nault dryly replied that her family was practically never out of mourning, some of their people having died almost every year recently.

Maman assumed an expression of sorrow and offered her

condolences to Madame Nault, who accepted them with a brief nod.

We were at once informed that Madame Nault was both niece and sister to archbishops, that she had been born Delilah Forget, and that young girls of good family did not have the opportunities of former times to marry well; advantageous matches were growing ever scarcer.

Maman also took on the airs of a lady of position: she remarked how true this all was, that we should like to prolong our visit with Madame Nault, but that we had many people and many things we must see during our trip to Montreal, that the time had come when we must return to our hotel. Then Maman added, as though it were quite incidental, that her husband held a post in the Ministry of Colonization. She spoke of one thing and another, and found ways to interlard frequent little phrases like "my husband – in the employ of the federal government" . . . "my husband – a civil servant of the state" . . . and I realized how much better received in society is a woman who boasts of her husband than one who is alone. This seemed to me unjust; I had never noticed that a man needed to talk of his wife in order to appear important.

Each time Maman said "my husband," Madame Nault thawed out a little more. And in the end she said that there could be no question of allowing visitors from Manitoba to sleep at a hotel. In the best of them, said she, women alone are exposed to serious dangers, and it did not take much, she hinted, to lose one's reputation in Montreal.

We spent three days in the apartment above the pharmacy. I do not think it was so much because our visit gave Madame Nault any great pleasure, yet all the same she would not hear of letting us go. "Never shall it be said," she explained,

"that I would not receive in my house a cousin from the West.
. . . Blood is thicker than water; never shall it be said . . ."
And without in the least enjoying it, we felt as though we were
prisoners, Maman and I, above the apothecary shop. Maman
put a good face on ill fortune, and the Naults went as far as
to offer us an expedition to Saint Joseph's Oratory. Its major
purpose, I imagine, was to see Brother André. That poor
wonder-worker sat from morning till night on a straight-backed
chair, his head in his hands, listening to the appeals and prayers
of the vast crowd filing past him. Many sought to be cured by
him; others wanted only to see if he looked like a saint; and
perhaps a few hoped for no more than his understanding. You
could not help feeling sorry for Brother André; almost the
whole while he kept his face a little hidden; one might have
thought that he had a headache, or that he himself felt sad at
not being understood by everyone. Certainly he had little time
to reply to all these people for every day, it would seem, there
came as many as on the day we went. Now it was Maman's
turn. She asked Brother André whether it was a great sin for a
married woman to leave on a journey without having obtained
her husband's consent. Perhaps Brother André did not hear
properly. He hastily replied to Maman: "Say a good prayer to
Saint Joseph, don't drink too much coffee, and have trust, always have trust."

Later we found other cousins in Montreal, and thank
heaven we did; otherwise Madame Nault would never have
yielded us our freedom, for "never shall it be said that she would
have left relatives alone and without advice in such a city. . . ."

When the pharmacy door shut behind us, Maman said
– I don't know why – "Poor Samuel!"

IV

I no longer remember all the other things we did in Montreal; but it was very tiring. We went to see an illuminated fountain at the other end of the city; then a waxworks museum; but the greater part of our time was spent, as I recall, in talking about the dead, about cousins unknown and of the third and fourth generations.

Then, one evening, I was sitting with Maman near a cabby in a horse-drawn trap, and we were progressing slowly along a low, dark road, where only puddles of water supplied what little light there was ahead of us. The turning wheels showered our faces and elegant jackets with gobbets of mud. We entered a tiny village – at least I thought it a village; a handful of feeble lights glimmered in the bushes. A little earlier, though – I remember now – the cabby had whispered something to Maman, who had pushed over toward me and cried, "Aren't you ashamed! And in front of a mere child! Be careful, sir; I have influential friends, and I could have you taken care of if I chose to make the effort."

Later on, when we were alone in the village, Maman warned me against men. "Now you see," said she, "how one must keep one's distance. . . ."

In this village, the name of which I have forgotten, it was raining, and the night was so dark I have rarely seen its like since. I was tired enough to fall asleep where I stood. Then my memory brings back to me a small, low-ceilinged room, very badly lighted by an oil lamp. Maman and I were surrounded by old maids in long skirts, which they were constantly pulling down over their ankles, black stockings, and collars stretching stiffly up their necks. Maman had half opened the jacket of her suit, by now somewhat wrinkled; beneath it she was wearing her lovely eggshell crepe de Chine blouse. And

Maman was explaining, "Your dear brother Edouard sends me to bring you his greetings and best wishes. . . ."

"Hasn't he gone over to the present government?" asked one of the spinsters from her place near a heavy wooden chest. "We heard he had sold out to the King of England. . . ."

"Come, Ursule, we are all subjects of the King of England, you yourself like me, like everyone in this country! What's more, your brother, by settling colonists in the West and laboring for the country's greatness, has not in the least denied his past as a French Canadian. . . ."

"He left when he was sixteen," complained another of the old maids, "and from that day to this we have received nothing from him but a single postcard, and that years ago. So he cannot have been as successful as you make out. If he had succeeded, he would have let us know. . . ."

"Perhaps he thought you no longer cared about him," said Maman. "How sensitive he is! . . . He imagined you felt no regret for him, but I know he still thought affectionately about you. And the proof is that I've known about you for years, you, my dear Ursule, and you, Aglaé. . . ."

"So much the better if that's the way of it," said Aglaé, who seemed the less spiteful. And she questioned Maman: "Out in your Manitoba, life is harsh and poverty-stricken, isn't it? You really have a wretched time out there?"

"Horrible! People in those parts freeze to death in their tracks," Ursule announced.

For a moment Maman hesitated, wondering how she should reply. She had already told several people that Manitoba was the most fertile country in the world. But this particular evening, having glanced at the three old ladies sitting quietly in the thick shadows of their home, to my great surprise Maman confirmed Ursule's indictment.

"Yes, Ursule dear, it is true that out there the climate is harsh, and the winds are relentless for all of us." She also described the vastness of the plains, the monotony of the West, and the boredom which overwhelmed us all!

I was dumbfounded; to Madame Nault, Maman had depicted us as better off than we were; here it was just the opposite, and it seemed to do no end of good to Papa's three elderly sisters, who at once appreciated their own wealth and happiness in their small, low-lying house. One of them – I think it was Aglaé – then remarked: "You see how it is with faraway places! You imagine them better than your own home . . . and sometimes they're a hundredfold worse! . . ."

Whereupon they all began to speak well of Papa. They reported that, even when a mere youngster, he had been proud by nature. Mother elaborated the point. "Your brother," said she, "would rather be cut alive into tiny bits than add an unjustified penny to his government expense account."

Ursule protested: it was silly, according to her, to put oneself out that much for the benefit of a government of English people. From then on they were all talking at once, Ursule prating about the English. Aglaé about Placide: "We must go see Placide . . ." she kept saying.

Yet Maman said, "Honesty is honesty, Ursule . . ." and the notion seized her of going to Saint Anne de Beaupré to pray for herself and for us all.

When we arrived there, Maman made me write a card to Papa, urging me to tell him that at last we had reached the true goal of our trip, which was to beg good Saint Anne to bless Papa's colonists and to obtain for him relief for his bronchitis. She advised me to add something of my own, "from my heart," reminding me how remarkable a man Papa was. However, since throughout our journey Maman had been discovering so many fine traits in Papa, I somehow felt I no longer knew him very well, and it embarrassed me to write him . . . almost as much as if it had been to a stranger.


v

Maman had been generous to Saint Anne. She bought her one of the biggest candles. Kneeling in front of her statue, she had had a long talk with Saint Anne. I've always thought that what Maman then asked of her was to cure her forever of the need for freedom – perhaps not too promptly, giving her time for another trip or two. . . .

I thought that now all our visits were over and that we should return straight home from the shrine. But no! Maman told me, "There is still Odile Constant. How I should love to find Odile Constant just once more!"

I asked her who on earth Odile Constant was.

"Odile," my mother replied, "was my dearest childhood friend when I was a little older than you,"

"But where shall we find Odile?"

"That," said Maman, "is always possible. If you really make an effort, you can always find an old friend, even if she's at the ends of the earth."

And thus it happened that we went to the village where Maman and Odile had been born. First we tried to get information at the priest's house. The pastor had heard that Odile Constant had entered a convent, but he knew not of what order. Then we ventured further, to the home of one of Odile's relatives, and he was able to tell us the name of the order, but not which house of that order; for fifteen years he had not laid eyes on her; she must have been transferred from one place to another; certainly she was still alive.

I was pleased to feel that we were almost "warm"; it was high time; we had very nearly no money left to continue our search; and besides, Maman seemed to set more store by this person than by all our cousins put together.

Once again we encountered sea gulls as we crossed a river, swimming around tufts of verdure that floated in the water. The Saint Lawrence was very lovely at this spot. We saw a big island; Maman told me it was Saint Helen's, which Champlain had given his bride, only twelve years old when he married her, and that there, on the island, he had let her grow up a few years. But despite this, it is Odile Constant's name which remains linked in my mind to this landscape.

The longer we searched, the more memories Maman recaptured of this little girl of earlier days; she even remembered the color of her eyes – hazelnut. And so, even had we never seen her in the flesh, we should all the same have rediscovered her.

"If God allows me to see Odile once more," said Maman, "I can say that I have satisfied my every wish."

I don't know why, but I still had it in my head that it was a little girl we were looking for so desperately.

At last at a convent door Maman inquired, "Could you let us see Odile – excuse me, I mean Sister Etienne du Sauveur. I am a very old childhood friend of hers. But don't tell her," Maman asked the portress! "I'd like so much to see whether Odile – I mean Sister Etienne du Sauveur – will recognize me."

The portress placed a finger over her lips; her sweet smile told us that the secret would be well kept, and noiselessly she went off to get Sister Etienne du Sauveur.

Maman and I were seated on chairs which, at our slightest movement, slipped a little on the gleaming parquet floor. It seemed to me that we avoided looking at each other; and if occasionally our eyes could not help meeting, we quickly averted our glances, as though we did not know each other very well. That must be the way of it when there are two of you awaiting the same good thing; perhaps each of you is afraid that, by too great a display of hope to the other, she will add to her disappointment, if that should be the outcome; or else perhaps you are embarrassed that both of you together should be awaiting happiness . . . I scarcely know. That is how it was – a kind of fear holding us by the throats – when we heard light footsteps coming toward us. Then in the doorway a nun with a pale face and feeble eyes – but gray they were, not hazelnut – was looking at us. Maman had urged upon me, "Don't say a word. Don't spoil it. Let me go alone to greet Odile."

The nun gave me a gentle, kindly glance, smiling at me as she did so, then looked at Maman. "Odile!" my mother called, as though to waken someone asleep.

At hearing this name, the nun trembled. Her two hands rose toward the crucifix hanging from her neck and she clasped it in both of them. Then she moved toward my mother; she took her by her arms and led her near a high window at the back of the parlor. She drew aside the curtains, to admit a better light into the room, and began to study Maman's face with a sort of eagerness to recognize her, which was even then utterly charming. Supposedly nuns forswear the affections of this world; ever since I saw Sister Etienne du Sauveur's face, I have believed that they don't always achieve so sad a perfection.

"Do you recognize me, Odile?" asked Maman in a thin little voice, which trembled with joyous fear.

Then the expression of the aged nun hurt me, so hard was she trying to look deep into Maman's face. It must have been difficult indeed to discover in an elderly, wrinkled face like Maman's a chubby-cheeked little girl with long braids. The old Sister was making so desperate an effort that her chin, her lips, even her hands were trembling. Finally she narrowed her scrutiny to Maman's very arched eyebrows, and it seemed as though they told her something; little by little there crept into her eyes a glow, at first of disbelief; then Sister Etienne cried out almost plaintively: "Good Lord! . . . Good Lord! Could it be my little Eveline?"

"Yes, it's I! It's Eveline!" Maman exclaimed, and threw herself in the nun's arms.

Then they both began to cry; they embraced, drew apart to stare once again into each other's faces. They kept saying to each other, weeping the while, "I knew you by your eyes . . ." and "Oh, but I knew you by the perfect arch of your eyebrows . . . no one but you ever ever had such beautifully curved eyebrows. . . ."

When they had had a good cry, they sat down facing each other, and Sister Etienne adjusted her headdress a bit, Maman having rumpled it somewhat when she held her tight. She said, all impatience, as though out of breath: "And now tell me, Eveline, my dear little Line, tell me about yourself. You must have had many an adventure! You're married! Are you happy? Tell me all about it."

"Yes," said Maman, "I married young. You understand, Odile, it was not a passionate love, a foolish love; I was marrying a man much older than I, a responsible man; but one by one I've discovered his fine qualities."

"If your husband has allowed you this fine trip, he's a generous man," Sister Etienne decided.

"Yes, very generous," said Maman.

"How happy I am! I'm sure that your husband is a very kindly man; he couldn't be otherwise. . . . You have children?"

"I've had nine," Maman said. "I've a daughter who is already married . . . another is a religious . . . a son long ago gone away . . . and I lost one child, Odile . . . a lovely little girl; she died so quickly . . ."

And they began to cry together over my little sister who had died of meningitis when she was four.

"But you," said Maman, wiping her eyes, "tell me about yourself. . . ."

"I," said Sister Etienne, "I have no history. . . . Tell me more about yourself. . . ."

"Well, then, my husband works for the Ministry of Colonization. He busies himself establishing European immigrants on our western lands. They're called homesteads."

"What a fine occupation!" exclaimed Sister Etienne. "So much more noble than business! I'm going to ask God to bless your husband's undertakings and also his colonist's efforts. . . . Couldn't you spend a day or two with me? Our Mother Provincial happens to be right here at the moment; I'll ask her permission. . . ."

"I'd certainly love it,"answered Maman, "but I must take the Transcontinental tomorrow for Winnipeg."

"The Transcontinental! For Winnipeg!" cried the nun, grasping her little cross. "And you say that as I might say I'm going to take the streetcar. . . . Dear, dear Line, go! Adventures will surely never frighten you. . . . Do you remember what I told you even then, thirty-eight years ago? 'You, my little Line, have been born to know great emotions. . . .'"

Maman then seemed to me constrained and ill at ease. "I sometimes wonder whether I go too far. . . ."

"No," Sister Etienne reassured her; "When God gives us a venturesome heart, it is in order that we may know better than others all the beautiful countries He has made. There are many ways of obeying God, Eveline . . . and freedom is one of the roads on which to journey toward Him. . . ."

And with her thumb she traced a little cross on each of our foreheads. After that she gave us medals, scapulars, and to both of us a picture of her patron saint.

In the entranceway to the convent, they both began to embrace each other. "To think that you have appeared and disappeared, like a comet!" Sister Etienne complained.

Maman begged her, "Pray for me, Odile. There are times when I sorely tempt Providence."

"Don't say that," the nun replied, as she studied Maman with her tired, kindly eyes. "I recognize them when I see beings set apart by Providence . . . set apart to their advantage . . . and you are such a one . . . such you are, my little Line. Dear, always trust in Providence."

And she added: "Eveline, I've lost all my own people long since. When they told me you were here to see me, it was four years since anyone had asked for me. Four years, Line, without a single visitor! . . ."

For a long while, standing in the convent doorway, she waved her hand after us, just like a little girl.

VI

On her way back to Winnipeg Maman seemed to grow older again. She thought of the Sister Superior at the Convent of Saint Anne-des-Chênes and said to me, "That sister had a strict look, none too amiable. If by any chance she's spoken harshly to Alicia, the child will never get over it, she's so timid!"

Then Maman began to worry about the food at the convent. "For the price I'm paying, it can't be very good. . . .

Agnès had very little appetite to begin with. Perhaps they haven't eaten anything for a whole month. . . ."

Maman, as it were, kept piling up her scruples. It's not worth going on a trip, thought I, if along the way one had to be prey to so many worries.

"Your father!" Maman would say. "Your poor father! Can you see him trying to get his own meals! He must have taken advantage of our absence to eat all sorts of indigestible things; he always does what he feels like when I'm not there to prevent him. . . . How slow this train is! You'd swear we're not moving at all. . . ."

We had traveled back across the country without seeing a thing except burned forests and burning brush piles. "This northern Ontario must surely be the dreariest country in the world," Maman complained.

She made a little conversation with a lady who was going as far as Great Slave Lake in Alberta. "Edouard, my husband, has a delicate stomach," Maman was saying. "He leads an exhausting life . . . a man of excessive probity. I'm afraid," she said, "that with me away he'll have undermined his health even more by staying up late and eating anything handy."

This lady answered severely, "If you were fearful of that, you had only not to leave your husband. . . . Why did you leave him?"

Maman watched the rain drench over the window. "Perhaps to become a better wife," she replied.

I instantly understood what she meant: it is when you leave your own that you truly find them, and you are happy about it; you wish them well; and you want also to be better yourself. But the lady journeying to Alberta had not the least idea what Maman meant. Her motive for traveling was very different. She was going west to settle an estate matter. Her aged and completely helpless husband could not stir from home. She explained dryly that she cared for him day and night and that she never left her "wifely duties."

Maman finally fell asleep, her hands over her skirt, which was all awry. As she slept, her mouth opened slightly and she began to wheeze a little in her slumber. Maman had always asked us to waken her when she wheezed . . . but she wasn't wheezing hard, and I let her rest a few minutes longer. . . . Little wrinkles began to appear on her face. Her head lolled a bit over her chest; I noticed that Maman had a slight double chin; other wrinkles took shape at the corners of her mouth. I saw that Maman was old. I was afraid. I woke her. I called out to her, "Maman! Maman!" as though she were far, very far away. And with a start, seeming not to recognize me, she cried, "What is it? What's the matter?"

Then she recognized me. She said to me, "Oh! It's you! I was dreaming that I had been left all alone in the world . . . that I had to wander from one end of the country to the other to find my children, who were scattered through all the provinces. . . ."

From the station we took the tram. We must have crossed the Provencher Bridge, but the windows were fogged over, and in any case neither of us thought of watching for the Red River.

There was a slight, chilling wind. We shivered a little, and Maman remarked that, after all, spring was less advanced in Manitoba than in the East, that Ursule would certainly be pleased over that. . . . Montreal had receded so far away that we might just as well never have been there. Out of our whole trip, it seemed to me the only thing I could still clearly see in my mind's eye was the big candle in front of Saint Anne. . . . From afar, when we got off at the corner of Rue

Desmeurons and Rue Deschambault, we saw that our house was all lighted up.

"Good heavens!" said Maman. "Can someone be sick?"

She quickened her pace, dragging me along so fast that I stumbled over my own feet.

We later learned that Papa had come home two weeks after we had left, upsetting Maman's plans; in her heart she had probably hoped she could make the whole long trip and resume her place at home before Papa even knew of our absence.

When he had entered the house, he had not noticed the letter Maman had left; he had rushed to the neighbors', worried and trembling, thinking we might all be sick and in the hospital. Madame Guilbert had been only too glad to give him the news: "What do you mean? Didn't Eveline tell you that she was leaving for Lower Canada with your little girl? . . . I thought you knew all about it . . . all the more so because she told me she had a pass. . . . What an amazing business . . . to have done such a thing!" But Papa did not lose his temper at Madame Guilbert's, as she had perhaps expected he would. He gathered his children together from their various temporary abodes. Once he had them around him, Papa did not say a word. He paced up and down. For ten days he had tramped through the house, along the downstairs passage, back and forth in the upstairs hall. The children had not dared say anything to him. It seemed that during those days everything took place at home in almost total silence – meals, dishwashing, reproaches, and all else.

They were sitting in the midst of this dreadful silence when Maman very quietly opened the door. Papa raised his eyes. He saw us. He turned pale, arose from his chair, and said, "Ah! At last! My gadabouts!"

I was afraid we'd be turned out of the house.

But then Maman walked over to my father; she was wearing her small blue straw hat adorned with a bunch of bright red grapes.

"Edouard," said my mother, "before you get to the well-deserved scolding, let me extend to you, in the name of your sisters and your brother Placide, their heartfelt greetings and all the good wishes they asked me to bring you. . . ."

"What! You even went . . ."

"Yes, Edouard, back into your past, as far as your childhood. . . . Without the past, what are we, Edouard?" she asked. "Severed plants, half alive! . . . That is what I've come to understand! . . ."

My father moved back, fumbling for the edge of his chair. And Maman continued. "It weighs a little on Ursule's heart that you should not have sent them any news for so long a time . . . but through my visit I think I have repaired the forgetfulness of the years. . . . Anyway, she is now fully restored to equanimity, thanks to hearing how important your work is. . . . I overheard her talking about it in the village. . . . Aglaé is sensitive by nature. . . . I liked your brother Placide right off. . . . His name suits him . . ."

I was looking at my mother; her eyes shone with sincerity, and – was it really possible? – she had grown young again. Before even taking off her jacket, which she merely unbuttoned, she was already launched on her tale. "Back there on what they call the 'ranks' the houses are not far from each other, as they are on our plains, but lined up in a row; they make one continuous village; beautiful trees, much larger and much sturdier than ours, border the roads; shadow and sunlight play over the white house fronts. Those Quebec houses, low-lying, with their narrow windows near the ground and their tall, pointed roofs perhaps do not let in as much daylight as ours in Manitoba, but they preserve better the warmth of memories. What a fine feeling when, with the lamps lighted, people's faces take on a look of friendship, and even the wood-work itself a tint of welcome! Then, in the silence, you can almost hear it remembering. . . . Perhaps," said Maman, "the generations of the dead still breathe around the living in that ancient land of Quebec! . . ."

Little by little we all drew close to Maman, the better to watch her eyes, which, in advance of her lips, foretold the sights she would describe. Because, before drawing them from her memory, her eyes caressed them, she smiled at them, playing gently the while with the small collar of artificial pearl around her neck.

A tear trickled down Papa's cheek, and he did not bother to brush it away. Timidly he asked about other details: Was the old apple tree still there, next the barn? Was some of the orchard left? And Maman filled in the picture for him, lifelike and touching. Upon her face her memories were like birds in full flight.

# THE WELL OF DUNREA

His strange life, so beautiful upon occasion, yet so hard and exacting, my father kept locked from our curiosity. He never said much about it, either to my mother or to me, even less to our neighbors. But he did talk about it to Agnès, on the syllables of whose name his voice lingered lovingly. Why and at what moment did he unburden so much of his heart to this young daughter of his, who was already oversensitive? She long kept as her own secret what my father had certainly told her not without considerable reticence. One evening she began repeating it to us. . . . Perhaps it was because we had just been complaining that Papa was none too companionable. "He was, indeed . . . he was. . . . Oh! if only you knew!" protested Agnès. And it was another strange thing that, while he was still alive, we spoke of my father in the past tense, perhaps thinking of another aspect of his personality, long since disappeared.

At the time in question, Papa was especially well pleased with the colony of White Russians or Ruthenians established at Dunrea. For a reason unkown to us he called them his "Little

Ruthenians." Of all the groups he had settled, this one prospered best. It had not yet been established for a full decade; a short enough time in which to build a happy settlement out of a handful of suspicious and illiterate immigrants, let alone clear the land, build houses, and even make God feel at home with icons and votive candles. Yet all this and much more had the Little Ruthenians accomplished. They were not a people absorbed in vexations, like the Dukhobors. Agnès seemed to remember that they, likewise, were Slavs, probably from Bucovina. Certainly the past counted for something in their lives -- a past deeply wretched -- but it was in the future, a wonderful and well-founded future, that the Little Ruthenians above all had faith when they came to Canada. And that was the sort of settler Papa liked: people facing forward, and not everlastingly whining over what they had had to leave behind.

Agnès told us that Papa had described his Dunrea settlement as a sort of paradise, and that was precisely the word he used -- a paradise.

He had to traverse ten miles of scrub, of swamp, of bad lands, constantly swept by the wind, to reach Dunrea. And suddenly there came into view well-shaped trees -- aspens, poplars, willows -- grouped in such a way that they seemed to constitute an oasis in the bareness of the plain. A little before arriving at this clump of greenery you could already hear, my father said, water flowing and gurgling. For among trees, so verdant and so healthy, almost hidden beneath them, ran a shallow little stream called the "Lost River." Could it indeed have been Papa -- so close-mouthed and sad -- who had furnished Agnès with all these details? And why her? No one but her? "Is it surprising that Papa so deeply loved this Lost River?" said Agnès. "Just think: he himself had created it, in a sense."

One day he had chanced to miss his way in the course of his rounds and had stumbled on the dried-up bed of this river; polished pebbles along its bottom and the placement of a few trees showed that here there had been water. And Papa fell in love with this nook of ground, once grassy and certainly charming; which with little care would recapture its former loveliness. He promised himself to settle some hard-working colonists here, good colonists, intelligent enough to glimpse what they could make of it with patience and a little imagination. Now the Little Ruthenians, when he brought them and showed them the bed of the Lost River, grasped at once what Papa liked about it, what he so clearly saw; they decided to remain there. And when Papa urged them to plant many trees near the Lost River, so as to hold the dampness in the soil, his Little Ruthenians had followed his suggestion. Thus from year to year the river yielded more water, and in places reached a depth of six feet. Thereafter, of their own accord, all sorts of other little trees began to grow along its shores and interlaced their branches and created a kind of tunnel of verdure through which flowed and sang the Lost River. For, even when rediscovered, it continued to be called the Lost River.

And it seems Papa told Agnès that what he liked best for his settlements was water. In that Saskatchewan, so lacking moisture, the resurrection of a river was a major business. "Fire," he had said, "and drought are my settlers' worst enemies; running water their greatest friend."

The Little Ruthenians, having placed their confidence in Papa's prediction that water would return here, had built their houses along the dry stream bed, to such good effect that ten years later, all their houses lay within the soft and murmurous protection of the trees and the water.

Papa, when he clambered out of his wagonette and hitched his mare Dolly to the edge of the well of Dunrea, beheld a ravishing landscape: scattered in the greenery lay a score of half-hidden little white houses with thatched roofs; there were as many outbuildings, equally clean, whitewashed every spring; and besides all this, beehives, dovecots, lean-tos of leaves and branches where in the heat of day the cows came for shelter; throughout the village there wandered freely flocks of white geese which filled it with their amusing clatter. And yet, Papa said, the houses were not really white; you realized that their gleaming color was softened by an extremely delicate tint, almost indiscernible, and due to the Ruthenian woman's covering their walls with a thin lime wash to which they had added a dose of bluing. In the windows, which were small and low, they had red geraniums in pots. And Papa said that after having jogged for miles through a dismal country-side of stiff grass and wild vegetation, nothing could be more attractive – yet more surprising, too – than Dunrea. Each time he saw it, he had to rub his eyes before he could credit them and thank God.

Maybe, also, when he set foot in Dunrea, Papa felt the great joy of having been right on that day when the future of this small corner of earth had revealed itself to him; and maybe his joy sprang even more from the fact that his Little Ruthenians had so well fulfilled his dream.

The moment he stepped down from his rig, Papa found himself surrounded with children; he patted their cheeks, tweaked their ears . . . a strange thing, for with his own children Papa never did such things. Yet perhaps those children, more than we, had confidence in Papa; after all, we often enough saw how tired and disappointed Papa looked; we knew he did not always succeed in his efforts; whereas these people believed him endowed with an almost supernatural power. Who can ever know what peace of mind, what certitude Papa felt among his Little Ruthenians? Isolated, far from any other village, not yet even speaking their neighbors' language, they must have relied wholly upon Papa, and the trust between them was total.

The geese, the hens, the young turkeys scattered in front of him as Papa walked along through the mass of flowers. He always said that when settlers planted flowers, it was a sure sign of success, of happiness. And among his Little Ruthenians sweet peas clambered on the fences, rows of tall sunflowers slowly turned their enormous faces; pale poppies spilled their smooth petals to be scattered by the wind. The women even set out flowers along the paths that led from the houses to the little privies; and it seems that Papa had laughed at this excess of adornment.

Papa, however, was a serious man, and his first concern was to look after the crops. Now for miles around the village it was always uniformly beautiful; the lands of the Little Ruthenians were free of weeds and well tilled; wheat, the various grains, alfalfa, lucerne, clover – all did splendidly. In their methods, too, the Little Ruthenians had followed Papa's ideas: he had advised them not to overburden the soil by trying for continuous heavy crops, but to rotate, to be patient, and they had heeded him. And maybe that is why he called his Dunrea settlement paradise. Was he not obeyed there as God had once been in His Eden? He was confident and had never yet been mistaken in all the things he had ordained for his Little Ruthenians. Yet these Little Ruthenians, Agnès elaborated, were not at all small; on the contrary, they were almost all of average stature, some of them even very tall and sturdy. Papa called them the Little Ruthenians for a reason unconnected with their size, but Agnès could not remember precisely what it was. Though, said she, it seems that in their intensely blue eyes there lingered something of childhood.

Papa made the rounds of the kitchen gardens, for he was interested in the rare vegetables the women raised there; there were garlic, cabbages, and turnips, as in all such gardens, but also dill, very large, succulent black beans, cucumbers, Papa said, as sweet as nuts, and a great many other things – melons, for instance; the Little Ruthenians were very fond of melons. Papa went here and there surrounded by an activity which hummed from every direction and yet remained invisible. He would go into one house, then another. On each threshold, the women came to kiss his hand, but Papa pulled it back; he was embarrassed by this gesture of submission. Followed by his interpreter, then, he was among his own. "For I forgot to explain," Agnès added, "Papa had had time only to learn a score or so of words in their dialect, and their English was not much better. Despite this, how well they understood each other! How they trusted the interpreter when he said: 'The gentleman sent by the government informs you that such and such measures should be taken . . .' or else, 'Boris Masaliuk respectfully inquires whether. . . .'"

Then the meal was ready. While the men talked business, the women had prepared the food in so great a silence that, each time, Papa was startled to hear soft words spoken near his ear: "If you please, Mr. Government, do us the great honor of coming to our table. . . ."

The men sat down; not the women, whose role now was to remain standing behind hosts and guests, attentive to pass them the various dishes. Was Papa sorry for them, was he fond of them, these silent, shy women, who hid their lovely tresses beneath kerchiefs and murmured, as they served the men, "If you please . . ."?

He had told Agnès that Ruthenian women's voices were the same as a murmuring of water and of silence. It is certain, though, that he would have preferred to see them seated at the same time as the men at their own table. This was the only fault he found with his Little Ruthenians – that they were absolute masters in their own families. Several times he was tempted to speak to them about this, to invite the women also to sit down at table . . . but he was not entirely at home.

Papa often spent a night at Dunrea. There he slept like a child. The women's voices were never high or screeching. They seemed happy. "But what does that prove?" Papa wondered. "The slaves of other days were certainly happier than their masters. Contentment is not necessarily the servant of justice." So the lot of the women at Dunrea was the only thing that upset him. He listened to them humming their babies to sleep . . . and soon he himself slipped into slumber as into a whole and deep submission. When he awoke, it was to the good smell of strong coffee which the women were preparing for him downstairs.

All that was too beautiful to last, my father would have said.

How did it happen that here alone peace and plenty reigned? Everywhere else his settlers encountered obstacles. Look how it was with his Dukhobors! Among them the Devil's malice borrowed the very teaching of Christ the better to sow confusion. Indeed, in their effort always to act as Christ would have done in our epoch, to fathom the meaning of His acts, of His parables, the Dukhobors committed folly after folly. Had they not decided, on the eve of winter, to set free all their domestic animals, because, said they, "Did not our God create all creatures free, beasts as well as men?"

But how were we to know what God wished us to do with the so many little lives committed to our care? thought Papa, and he had said this to his Dukhobors, that one must not too greatly rack one's brain over this subject, that the important thing was not to mistreat any animal. None the less, the Dukhobors remained tortured by the idea that they must not infringe any of God's wishes . . . and they set free their flocks; which meant that they had to drive them out of their stables and pens.

The poor animals, upset and troubled, wanted to return to their captivity. But they were prevented. The snow came. The animals found nothing to eat; they almost all perished; in the spring only a handful – and they no more than fearful skeletons – came back toward the dwellings of men. Thus among the Dukhobors the young children suffered a series of illnesses for lack of milk. Among the Mennonites it was folly of another sort. Many were the misfortunes in Saskatchewan in those days . . . and almost always through excess of good will, through eagerness to understand God perfectly.

And why was Dunrea alone spared? The men there were well behaved, true enough; they believed in God. Perhaps, even, they believed that God loved them better than He loved the Dukhobors and the Mennonites; this notion apart, they seemed to dwell in wisdom.

And Papa himself began to wonder why God seemed to love the Little Ruthenians better than the others. He was careful not to confuse their simple, naïve minds; he did not too severely try their good will. And from then on Papa felt a kind of anxiety. He blamed himself for having certainly been too proud of Dunrea.

Whenever influential government people, top men from the Ministry of Colonization, asked to visit settlements, Papa always took them to Dunrea. And Dunrea helped his career, earned him consideration. The railroad companies sent photographers to make pictures of the Lost River; and the Canadian Pacific Railway produced a large number of Dunrea photos, sending them to places all over the world, to Poland, to Romania, to attract immigrants. For the C.P.R. made a great deal of money from the transportation of immigrants. My father one day met a poor Czech who confided to him that he had come to Canada only because he had seen a very tempting poster: a river, golden wheat, houses "just like those at home . . ." and now this Czech was working in a mine.

When Agnès told us this, we understood why Papa hated all lies, and even lies by admission; why he suffered so much because Maman dressed things up a bit; but that is another story. . . . At Dunrea, despite Papa's fears, the wheat continued to grow, the fine cattle to multiply. And since they prospered, the Little Ruthenians believed themselves better and better loved by God. They thanked Him for rains that came when they were needed, for sunshine in due season. They had no least expectation that God's gentle hand would ever weigh heavily upon them.

II

Delicate and sweethearted as she was, how could Agnès have kept to herself so long the spectacle she at last described to us? In those days, Papa had told her, prairie fires were always smoldering somewhere in Saskatchewan. This province, so lacking in rainfall and so windy, was truly the land of fire. So dry was it that the sun alone, playing on straw or a bottle shard, could set the prairie aflame! And if the slightest active breath of air should then make known its presence, at once the fire began to run like the wind itself. Now the wind in this part of the world was already a furious, mad thing, which beat the harvests to the ground, uprooted trees, and sometimes tore the roofs from buildings. Yet satanic as it was, it still left behind it the grasses cropped close to the soil, some living thing. But behind the fire, there remained nothing save the carcasses of young fawns, of rabbits pursued by the flames, overtaken by them, sometimes fallen dead in full flight. . . . And for a long time these carcasses poisoned the air, for in the place where fire had passed, even the birds of prey took care not to come to eat the eyes of the dead animals. This was a not uncommon sight in many areas of Saskatchewan, and a man's heart could little bear to see a ruin so complete.

The Little Ruthenians had always been very careful of fire; when, from time to time, they had to burn stumps or weeds, they waited for a very calm day; and once the fire had done its work, they put it out by scattering the coals and then covering them with moist earth. Moreover, in their ever-damp oasis, within earshot of the murmuring Lost River, how could they truly have feared fire?

Now that particular summer was burning dry. Even in the Lost River the water level went down several feet. And a fire started, probably ignited by nothing more than the sun, twenty miles north of Dunrea. At first the wind drove it in another direction. My father was camping eighteen miles farther on, in a region he was looking over with a party of surveyors. During the night he awoke. The wind had changed. It was stronger and laden with an acrid smoke which hurt eyes and throat. A little later a messenger arrived on horseback. He said the fire was moving toward Dunrea. My father jumped into the wagonette; he made no attempt to follow the road, which was far from straight in that part of the country; as much as possible he took short cuts through the brambles and small, dried-up swamps. Dolly obeyed him faithfully, even though she was wounded by the sharp point of the briars. Behind him, as he crossed these gloomy stretches of scrub, my father saw the fire following him from afar, and he heard its rumble. He prayed for the Lost River. He hoped for another change in the wind, which would sweep the fire elsewhere, no matter in what direction save toward Dunrea. This sort of prayer, he admitted, was perhaps not a good prayer. Indeed, why pray for his Ruthenians rather than for the poor, lonely farms along the Lost River road? Is the misfortune that strikes those one loves greater, my father asked himself, than that which strikes those unknown to us?

Arriving at Dunrea, he ordered the men to take their horses and plows and quickly to turn under a wide belt around the village. He set other men to digging ditches. The sky had become bright red . . . and that helped along the work, since one could see by it as though it were broad daylight. But how strange a daylight! What a dreadful glow silhouetted the terrified animals, the running men, each gesture and attitude of every moving shadow, but without disclosing their features, so that all these living beings looked like black cutouts against the horizon! Then the fire grew more intense; it divided and came from two directions at once toward the settlement. Papa ordered the women to leave, taking with them the children and old people. "The fewest things possible," he cried out to them. "Quick! . . . Leave your furniture . . . leave everything. . . ."

How astounded he now was at these women he had believed to be so docile! At first they did not want to leave the trenches they were digging alongside their men. Papa ran from

one to the other, even grasping a few of them by the shoulders
and shaking them a little.

Oh, those stubborn women! Once in their houses, they
began collecting a hundred useless articles: mattresses, quilts,
saucepans. "Is this the time to think of such things?" Papa
angrily called out to them.

But they kept going back into their houses, one to collect
her coffeepot, another a fine porcelain cup.

The farm wagons, the small two-wheeled carts, the
buggies were piled high with domestic goods; upon these were
perched the children, torn from their sleep, and now crying
miserably, and hens that kept flying off, and young pigs.
Women were hitching cows to the wagon tails. Never, so long
as there remained a single movable object, would these insub-
ordinate women have agreed to go. Papa ran about, whipping
the horses at the head of the caravan. Terrified, they rushed
toward the gap to the south, between the columns of fire
which little by little were closing in on each other. Then Papa
had the idea of setting fire to the crops to the north of the
village. In this way fire would advance toward fire, and perhaps
it would burn itself out. Such tactics had already succeeded on
other occasions. He called Jan Sibulesky, one of the Little
Ruthenians in whom he had always placed the greatest
confidence, a man of judgment, quick to grasp what was sensible and make a rational choice.

"Quick," said my father to Jan Sibulesky, "take with you
three or four men and, as soon as you can, set fire to the
corners of all the wheat fields."

This was the moment when the Little Ruthenians gave
every semblance of no longer understanding Papa. Jan as much
as the others! Oh, the obstinate, greedy, silly men! In their
own country they had possessed nothing – or so very little: a

skimpy acre or two on the arid slopes of the Carpathians to feed an entire family; and they had left that behind them without too great pain. But now that they had all sorts of things – hay, sugar beets, wonderful wheat, full barns, really everything – they would not part with the least trifle.

"But if you want to keep everything, you'll lose everything," Papa told them.

And my father turned into something like a madman. He waved his arms, he shouted insults, thinking perhaps that the Little Ruthenians would at least understand those words. But the foolish wretches through all the thick smoke madly concentrated on pushing their plows around the settlement. Others carried water from the river to the houses to wet down the walls; still others drew pailfuls from the communal well, in the center of the village, which was deep and almost icy. Did they think that this water, so cold it clouded the outside of the pail, would serve better to cool the atmosphere than the water from the river? Then Papa tried to go by himself to set fire to the harvest, but the Little Ruthenians forcibly prevented him. Thus Papa realized that they had perfectly well understood his orders, that henceforth he was alone among his own people, as they were on their own against him. This loneliness in the face of danger made him despair. The heat was increasing. Occasional brands of fire flew over the village. A powerful roar filled the air. And everything was in fearful disorder; no longer was there anyone in charge, any obedience. Each man was wearing himself out in individual effort; a few simply awaited the fire, ax in hand. Then the flames at a single bound cleared one of the trenches; they took hold of a thatched roof; in an instant the house glowed with inner light. All was lost.

"Go, go!" Papa cried to the men. "You've only enough time to save yourselves!"

STREET OF RICHES

I have often envisioned Papa as he must have appeared that night, very tall with his arms stretched toward the sky, which outlined him also in black. What a terrible silhouette!

But now the Little Ruthenians were trying to save the burning house. So Papa moved toward them threateningly. He raised his hand, showed them the glowing heavens, and, in their own tongue, he asked them: "Don't you know what that means?"

All equally bewildered, they raised their heads toward the nightmare glow above them. Papa said that they looked like stupid birds turning their heads in unison toward an incomprehensible sign. And in their own tongue Papa told them what the sign meant: "The wrath of God! Do you understand? It is God's wrath!"

Then there took place something infinitely cruel. Understanding at last, all the men made ready to go – all except that Jan Sibulesky whom father had loved and often singled out as an example because of his never-failing judgment. Abruptly Jan rushed toward the chapel and emerged from it holding an icon of the Virgin. His icon in front of him like a shield, he walked toward the burning house. Papa at once understood what Jan was going to do. The flames illumined his face, his mouth, his forehead hardened in unshakable purpose, his blond beard, his blue eyes; in the full light big Jan marched forward, utterly visible; just as visible was the icon he carried, the icon of a Madonna with tender, childlike features. Thus brilliantly lighted, the eyes of the image shone as though they were alive.

"Stop, you idiot!" my father cried out to Jan.

But it was now a long while since anyone had obeyed him. His great mistake obviously, had been to speak of God's wrath. All his life my father believed that there had lain his crime: to have interpreted God, in a sense to have judged

Him. Jan continued toward the flames, singing a hymn and holding the holy image just below his harsh face.

"You're going to die," Papa told him. "Stop him! Stop the poor fool!" he begged the others.

But they all stood like spectators, in a living hedgerow, and probably at that moment they were very curious about God and about Jan; so avid with curiosity that they were stripped of all other thoughts. The words of the canticle resounded for another moment above the crackling of the flames; then suddenly they changed into an appalling cry. Never could Papa erase from his memory, right upon the heels of the tones of prayer, this roar of horror. A blazing beam had tumbled upon Jan Sibulesky. The men who had been so intense upon miracles at last made up their minds to leave – and in a stampede. They sprang astride their horses, urging them on with sharp cries; they clambered onto the seats of the two-wheeled traps; they dashed out of the village, jostling each other. Papa begged them, as they passed him, to call out their names, for he could no longer recognize faces in the smoke, and he wanted to reassure himself that none of the Little Ruthenians would be left behind. "Get south'" he yelled at each outfit as it passed by. In that direction, between the walls of fire, there was still a gap which, minute by minute, was visibly closing.

At last Papa jumped into his wagonette and, by the sound of the galloping horses, he tried to follow the caravan now hidden in the smoke. His vehicle, however, was too heavy to make enough speed over the stones and clods of earth. Papa at a bound put himself astride Dolly; then he got out his penknife and began to slash at the leather traces that attached the wagonette to the mare, reducing her speed. The traces were tough and hard to sever, but at last one came free, and then the other. Dolly went faster. The fire, though, was already raging here and there on the only route still open. Papa saw that Dolly by herself could get through quickly enough not to be burned, but that, burdened with a man, she certainly could not. From far up ahead one of the Ruthenians cried out to him to hurry. Papa called back that he needn't worry, he was coming. That was the last human voice he heard that night. Standing beside Dolly he gave her his orders: "Go . . . go . . . As for me, I still have the well of Dunrea; there – if I can get back to it – I'll be safe. . . . And I'm too tired, really too tired to go much farther. . . . The well will give me a bit of rest. . . ."

But that night no one was to obey him, not even his gentle, his obedient Dolly, for whom Papa, whenever he left Winnipeg on the way to his settlement, always took with him titbits and lump sugar.

So he raised his whip and struck Dolly a blow, on her most sensitive part, over the eyes. She went off neighing with pain and reproach. And, running, bending double to avoid the flames, Papa regained the center of Dunrea. His hair, his beard, his eyebrows were singed from the heat. He breathed as little as possible, holding a damp handkerchief over his mouth. He reached the edge of the well. Grasping the rope used to haul up the pails of water, Papa slid down into the deep, cool interior. He lowered himself to the level of the water. Almost at once the roar of the flames surrounded everything. All around the well the grass was afire. The rope likewise began to burn; Papa saw it come apart, strand by strand, in little spirals of ash. Quickly he pried out bricks, which were only loosely imbedded in the lining of the well; he dug himself a sort of niche, where he succeeded in finding a certain support. Then he cut the rope as high as he could. At just that moment he saw a shadow over the well opening, in perfect outline. He

was greeted by a long-drawn-out neigh. "Oh Dolly!" cried my
father, "Go . . . Go!" He ripped free a brick which he hurled
at Dolly's head. Papa said that she leaned in to see whence
came the furious voice and projectile. Then she reared and
raised herself to a great height, head and mane erect. Papa
began to smell the odor of burned flesh.

And he told how the inside of the well became broiling
hot, the air so unbreathable that he had to go lower yet. He
did it with the help of the rope, which he had tied to a stone
projecting from the inner wall. He slipped into the water up
to his knees, then to his waist. Half his body was freezing and
numbed, while upon his head rained sparks of fire . . . and he
thought that the end had really come. Papa said that he had
been sure he was dead because suddenly nothing mattered to
him any more. This was what gave him the deepest anguish
when he thought back afterward: that everything, in the depth
of the well, had become so dismal, so smothered, so extraordinarily silent. He had not thought of us; all he felt was
quiet, so great a quiet that it was beyond resisting. These were
his own words: "Neither regrets, nor hope, nor desires: a state
of complete quiet." At the bottom of the well he barely could
succeed in remembering life, having been alive. And how
could he have the least taste for any return from so deep an
indifference! Papa, believing himself dead, was a trifle astonished that death should be so gloomy, glacial, empty . . . and
so reposing . . . that in death there should no longer be any
affection possible. Within him there was a desert, just as above
his head – in Dunrea there was also a desert.

Papa said that then, in this absence of life, he had seen
Agnès, come to wait for him as she always came to meet the
tram that brought our father back from Winnipeg. He said
that he had seen her at the trolley stop, at the end of our short

Rue Deschambault, and that close to her stood our old collie dog, which always accompanied Agnès. Such was the vision that in the end had penetrated so far to find Papa, in his quiet; regret at seeing the child and her dog futilely waiting day after day, for weeks and months – here was what brought his dead soul back to life. He had rediscovered the language of other days, faraway words. "Go home, you and the dog – back to the house!" he had tried to tell Agnès. And this word "house," which his lips pronounced, none the less only awakened an extreme astonishment in the depths of his brain. "The house! Whose house? Why houses? . . ." And again he tried to persuade the stubborn child, standing at the street corner, despite a cold wind, and shivering, to go home. "There's no use waiting for me; I'm already dead. Don't you understand? To be dead is to have no more love – at last!" But Agnès answered Papa in the bottom of the well: "You'll come back; I know it . . . maybe even in this next tram. . . ."

And Papa had been startled at hearing himself speak; the sound of his voice had made him understand that he was not dead. Because of the child at the end of the street, he made an enormous effort to fasten himself with the rope to the wall of the well. He had fainted.

The next morning the Little Ruthenians found him in the well.

When Papa opened his eyes on the desolation that was now the Lost River, he believed in Hell. Curiously, it was not with the furnace of the night before, with the outcries, with the unfollowed orders, that he was to associate Hell, but with this – a thick silence, almost inviolable, a dismal land, black everywhere, a dreadful death.

Raising himself up on the charred soil where they had laid him, Papa tried to give courage to his Little Ruthenians;

since they had not lost their lives, they had not lost the essential thing. Neither he himself, however, nor the Little Ruthenians, had much further use for this essential thing. They said that they had, all the same, lost their lives, at least ten years of their lives. . . . And Papa remembered to ask about the women: "Are they all safe?" "Yes," the Little Ruthenians replied, "they are all safe, but weeping for their dear houses, their oaken chests, their chests full of fine linen. . . ."

Papa returned among us . . . and yet did he ever return? Appalled at his appearance, Maman asked him, "Has something happened to you, Edouard? What on earth has happened to you?"

But Papa merely put her off with an inconsequential account of what had taken place, how he had lost a settlement. For a long time that was all he ever admitted. Only to Agnès, when one evening she came and sat close beside him and looked at him tenderly – she was not afraid, never was afraid of his half-burned eyebrows – only to Agnès did he tell how he had once meddled with the business of explaining God to men; perhaps it was a day – when he regretted not having remained in the depths of the well. . . . When Lazarus emerged from the grave, we have no knowledge that he was ever gay.

Still, there remained this most curious thing: Papa, become, as it were, a stranger to joy, so far removed from it that he was almost unable to recognize it in a human countenance, was nevertheless, sensitive to suffering.

Oh, here indeed was something that troubled us: when we laughed, when on occasion we succeeded in being happy, Papa was astounded! But let a misfortune, a sorrow strike one of us, then we saw Papa come alive . . . return to us . . . suffer all the more!

# ALICIA

I must tell the story of Alicia; certainly it left the greatest mark upon my life; but how dearly it costs me!

Our Alicia with her huge dark blue eyes! And the so-strange contrast in her between those eyes and her coal-black hair! From Maman she had inherited also the loveliest eyebrows I remember ever to have seen, so roundly arched, so high and sharply delineated that they gave her glance an expression of amazement, of pain at the spectacle of life. She was still herself, with her pale, slender face; yet no, it was no longer Alicia. For already she no longer recognized those she so deeply loved; me alone, at times, she still knew. Her strange eyes would come back from so far way that to see them return filled me with dread; then she would look at me, smile at me as before; maybe she would even kiss me in the joy of rediscovering me; but she clung to me too tightly; and of her, of Alicia, I now was frightened! Then she would go back to where she had come from; her eyes would lose us all, relatives, friends, little sister. There would be no one but herself imprisoned within her queer look. Even then I could imagine how terrible it must be to be all alone within oneself.

"Whatever is the matter with Alicia?" I would go ask Maman.

At home we were always very reluctant to cry where anyone could see us. But how very often, at that time, when I went into the kitchen and found Maman alone, I caught her wiping her eyes with the corner of her apron! And she would hastily become a person with a great deal to do, who cannot be bothered. I would insist, "What's the matter with Alicia?"

They – I mean the grownups – were protecting me from the truth. They told me Alicia had nothing the matter with her. Is this what constitutes childhood: by means of lies, to be kept in a world apart? But *they* could not prevent my seeking; and seeking by myself alone, without help, kept bringing me back into their world.

It was summer. A hotter, more brilliant summer I do not think there ever was on Rue Deschambault. We were as though readied for happiness, with our trees full of fruit, flowers all around the house, the lawn well cropped. If I remember that summer so well, certainly it was because the season was so out of joint, so little in tune with our thoughts. Alicia alone seemed not to be aware of this contrast. She, who was the cause of our misery, withdrew from it as though she had no part in it; almost all the time she was humming.

One day she went up to the attic.

Constantly we would ask each other, worried, as though concerned about a tiny little child who had eluded our watchfulness, "Where is Alicia?"

And almost every day I would find the answer, "In the attic."

Once, though, it took me a long while to discover her. She had hidden herself in the depths of a dark cupboard, and when I at last found her, she was holding her head in her hands; this time she was crying.

Yet how was it that, having found her in an attitude which indicated she wanted to play hide-and-seek with me, I had no feeling that this was a game, nor any taste to join in it? In the past she and I had often played at hiding from each other; yet when we found each other once more, it was to bubble with laughter or accuse each other of cheating.

"Where is Alicia?" Maman would ask me.

And I would tell her; I would say: "Today she's braiding flowers and singing."

Why was it so sad to see Alicia spend hours weaving flowers together to make necklaces and bracelets for her adornment? Merely because she was no longer a little girl? . . .

One day in the attic Alicia put on a long white dress; around her waist she fastened a wide, sky-blue belt; in her hair she tucked some roses. I had never seen her look so lovely; and why was it sad to see her thus? She leaned out of the garret window toward the street and began scattering petals from the roses over the heads of the occasional passers-by. And she sang plaintively, "Here are flowers . . . good people. . . . Here are roses for you who walk by! . . ."

I don't know why, but I felt obliged to go tell Maman that Alicia was throwing roses at the heads of the people in the street; one might have thought it somehow disgraced us.

"Go back up to her; try to distract her," said Maman. "Get her away from the window."

That day, however, Alicia did not even know me. When I tried to make her move, she abruptly gave me a malignant glance and began screaming "Judas! Judas!" at me. I was terribly afraid of Alicia, and ran off trembling. Yet it was only yesterday that Alicia had been taking care of me. She was responsible for me when Maman was very tired or when, wanting a full afternoon undisturbed to tackle some major sewing project, she handed me over to Alicia. She would say, "Alicia, don't you want to take the little one for a walk? Will you look out for her?" Many an older sister would not have enjoyed constantly to be encumbered with a little girl like me. But Alicia never wounded me by seeming to be bored at the prospect of having to look after me.

It's true that I gave her the least possible trouble. We would leave the house together, and I was enchanted at seeing that we always took to the wilder side of the street. Never did we go – Alicia and I – toward town; that did not interest us; we would follow the narrow wooden sidewalk as far as the last house on our street. Then we would continue on across the fields, soon reaching our little grove of black oaks. In my childhood I thought this grove huge; I believed it a forest. . . . I have long realized that it was merely a largish clump of trees none too close together; it could not even wholly hide from us the distant gable of our house. No matter; it was among these small black oaks that I most fully felt the slightly dangerous mystery, the attractions, the solemn joy of being in the woods. Alicia helped me maintain this feeling. She would say to me, as we drew near our little oaks, "See! They look just like conspirators wrapped in their long, black coats." Then we forgot that the oaks were conspirators; we stretched out on the grass and watched the acorns fall, which sometimes landed right on our noses, when we had not been quick enough to dodge them. We could spend hours without exchanging a word. Already Alicia's thoughts, though, were not always happy. One day, having announced to her that when I grew up, I would do fine and beautiful things, Alicia told me sadly, "One says that, and then one never accomplishes anything except paltry things of no account."

"But mine will be great!"

Then, as though I were ill, exposed to I know not what, Alicia took me in her arms; she rocked me under a small oak tree rustling quietly in the wind, and I felt as though I were being cradled by the tree, the sky, by an inexhaustible tenderness. Yet when I pulled myself a little away from Alicia, I saw she was crying.

She told me: "You see, what I should like is that no one suffer. I'd like to spend my life preventing sorrow from touching people – Papa, Maman first of all, and then – oh, everyone. Why not everyone? How much hurt is in the world!"

Whereupon she had again clasped me in her arms, saying, "I'll defend you. I won't let them do you harm!"

II

Now, however, she did not see how miserable we were. She remembered no one of us. She was our greatest unhappiness. When visitors came, we tried to hide her. There were some of our acquaintances and friends who still asked after her; the majority pretended they no longer included her in our number; yet some few still asked Maman, "And your daughter Alicia?"

Maman would explain how Alicia had been stricken with a fever which had, as it were, consumed her, adding what the doctors said of such illnesses: either they killed you or else the sequel was worse than death. . . .

And I would go off into a corner of the garden to ponder her words. Whatever could be worse than death? I suppose I preferred to keep Alicia, unhappy, than to see her die. I was afraid lest now they wanted her dead. And from then on it was I who kept saying, "I'll defend Alicia. I won't let them do her any harm. . . ." But one day she bit me savagely, and Maman noticed it.

She was trembling while she questioned me: "She hurt you? And – before this – has it ever happened that she hurt you?"

I could not wholly deny it; I was filled with bottomless terror.

Then it was that *they* decided to send Alicia away. *They* did not tell me the truth; *they* arranged the truth; *they* wholly transformed it. To all my desperate insistence – "Where is Alicia" – *they* replied that she was in good hands, that perhaps she would return to health, that I must pray for her. And then, from time to time, I would still ask, "What's the matter with Alicia?"

And Maman, who had been so patient with me, put me off rather harshly. "Don't you see I'm so busy I don't know what I'm about? Leave me alone!" said Maman.

One day Papa and Maman were talking confidentially. I could tell by their faces when what they had to say was of interest to me. I pretended to be busy coloring my picture book. Papa and Maman glanced at me, then continued their conversation.

"It's a chance worth taking," Papa was saying. "Alicia loved her so! . . ."

"But she's only a child! . . . And to take her to such a place, Edouard!" said Maman. "Do you realize? . . ."

But Papa replied, "She was so fond of the baby! The joy of seeing her again, perhaps. . . . Shouldn't we try everything?"

"At her age," and Maman indicated me with a motion of her chin, "she could be marked for life. . . ."

Papa insisted, "Remember how she loved her. If anyone can still do anything, it's surely our baby. . . . Only she can work the miracle . . . ."

Then, realizing that they expected a miracle of me. I scuttled off and hid beneath the lower branches of the balsams. They hunted for me all afternoon; and when by evening they had not yet found me, they kept calling from the house, "Petite Misère! Christine!"

Underneath the evergreens in the darkness I was thinking of the picnics we so often had had together – just the two of us, Alicia and I. I presume that she had retained from childhood that need, that deep taste for independence, since we – we children – have so little true independence. In any case, to her as to me, nothing seemed less agreeable, more tiresome, than to sit down at the table for a meal. Thus quite often we persuaded Maman to give us permission to take some bread and jam, which we then consumed – was it not strange? – in a cornfield lying a little beyond the oak grove on the edge of the diminutive Seine River. This spot was not a bit comfortable; it afforded us no least level space on which to spread out our food, and obviously there was no view. None the less, between the high rows of corn, Alicia and I had long taken delight in feeling as though we were closed in, well protected, wholly hidden. We spent hours there, not in the least embarrassed by the fact that we had just enough room to sit down – to stoop, rather – between the close-planted stalks. The rustling of the big leaves, the occasional cry of a bird in the field, a sound as of rippling water which the wind made as it brushed the young ears, their silk, which we tore off to make ourselves beards or mustaches – to us all this was pleasure and high fun! Moreover – and this gave us a warm feeling of security – no one could possibly have come near us without our hearing them. In the cornfield we were as in a fortress, well protected against others by the extreme pliancy of the stalks which, by the least change in the tone of their crackling, would have betrayed any invasion of our domain. Maman, however, eventually learned where we spent our afternoons; she had already begun to be anxious.

"In the corn! Why always go eat in the corn when there are such lovely other places?"

### III

Very early in the morning Maman and I left to go there.

On the way I asked, "Have you locked Alicia up?"

Maman tried to laugh. "Locked up! What an idea! Of course not: she's in very good hands. She's being cared for by the best doctors."

But the small town we came to had a dismal look, unlike any other town. At least, so I saw it. Perhaps it was because of me. Since those days I have noticed that our thoughts have a great and curious power over things; on certain days they can make seem beautiful some wretched gray hovel; yet it can also happen that they make very ugly something that is not such in itself. This town seemed to me silent, bored, and somehow ill at ease in the sunlight. On a low hill a little outside the town, there towered a large, high building still more silent and more severe than all the rest; it was to this structure that we bent our steps. But I should mention that on arriving Maman had to ask directions, and she asked with a blush, in a low, unhappy tone. Now that we knew our way, we approached the high brick building and we soon became aware that it was placed in the midst of rather handsome grounds, with paths, seats, even swings, and many trees. But whence came the impression that despite these grounds, this structure had no means of exit anywhere? Maybe because of an iron fence all round it. . . .

I remembered the field of corn; there one was locked in, true enough, but it was a very different thing! . . . Might not freedom reside in remaining within a very tiny space which you can leave if you have a mind to?

And how many trips had I already made with Maman. I thought to myself; some of them the finest in the world, in which I saw everything around me, others so sad they hid from me every vista. How strange is travel!

We knocked on a heavy door. A most impassive woman received us in a parlor. I say parlor for lack of a better word, since it was much better furnished than a convent or priest's house parlor. There was reading matter scattered about, good easy chairs gaily upholstered in chintz. Nevertheless, the idea would not have occurred to me to call this room a living room; you could be there only for the purpose of waiting . . . waiting. . . . Such was the message of its silence; and yet all sorts of tiny sounds reached you from afar, like soft, almost fleeting footsteps, and the noise of keys: keys being turned in locks, keys swinging on a chain tied around the waist. Then I heard a peal of laughter, brief but frightening. I quickly held my hands to my ears. Maman seemed not to have heard it. She did not even notice how greatly I was terrified. Maman must have been deeply saddened no longer even to notice my own sadness. *They* say that sorrow brings people together. This is not always true; that day sorrow built a round wall tight closed about Maman as she sat erect on a straight-backed chair.

Then we heard footsteps coming toward us. The door opened. In the company of a blue-uniformed woman Alicia stood on the threshold. I say Alicia also for want of anything better. For it could not be Alicia who stood that way, her head bent, her body sagging as though broken, broken in I know not what abominable fashion!

And I wanted to cry out to the woman, to the building, to the whole red town, "What have you done to Alicia?"

The woman in uniform told Maman that *she* was much better, that obviously one could not expect too much, but that there was progress; then she left us.

Alicia, having sat down, remained motionless, unseeing.

"Alicia," said Maman, ever so gently, "don't you recognize me?" And Maman named herself: "Your mother . . ." yet so embarrassed at having to say it that, like a wax taper, she seemed to burn and then melt away. . . .

Alicia lifted her head a little; her eyes gave Maman a sideways glance; they swept over Maman's face as though it were that of a pleasant stranger . . . and moved on elsewhere. . . .

It's curious, but only then did I understand the words that, for some time now, Maman occasionally murmured to herself: "In my grave . . . I wish I were in my grave! . . ."

Then she encouraged me with a brief gesture, not overpersuasive, as though she thought, "Do try – you – to work the miracle."

I slipped out of my chair. I moved close to Alicia. I put my arms around her waist, and I, also, called out to her, "Alicia!"

She smiled at me then, but it was like the smile of a small child, who recognizes only very vaguely, by their faces, by their voices, those who love her. And my heart was broken; I know it must have been broken; I had no more courage left for the miracle. I let my head fall over Alicia's knees and I began to cry, suddenly remembering the rustle of the corn leaves above us.

Then I felt Alicia's hands, which softly stroked my wet cheek, as though to take stock of something inexplicable, very strange; and as though this hand were going forth to meet a habit long forgotten and little by little rediscovered, it began to stroke my temples and my hair.

I turned my head on Alicia's knees. Her eyes were straining, focusing on a problem so absorbing that their pupils betrayed no slightest motion. You would have thought that a light from deep within her was striving to reach her eyes; and that made me think of long dark corridors through which one passes with a lamp in one's hand. . . . Had Alicia, then, so long a distance to traverse, alone in those black corridors? And was it recollection – that tiny glow which from time to time I saw shine behind her eyes?

Abruptly the light shone brighter there. With her small lamp shining in her hand, Alicia must have been nearing the end of the passage; thoughts, real thoughts, flitted across her face, but like veiled, uncertain passengers. Oh, how deeply stirring it is to behold a soul returning to a human countenance!

Alicia held me with her eyes. She looked at me intensely, smiled at me, found my name. She even spoke to me: "The Little One! It's you! Where on earth did you come from all by yourself?"

And then she cried out: "You've come to get me! It's you who have come to get me! . . . I knew you'd come! . . ."

And joy flooded her face as though it were the sun itself. Was it not a thing to marvel at? Returning to life, Alicia's soul first of all found joy! As though the soul had been made for joy! . . .

But at once her lips, her hands began to tremble! Why, immediately after joy, did despair cast itself upon her? Never before had I seen despair, and yet I recognized it. Such it surely was: a moment of lucidity, when you see your life and the harm you do others, all their unhappiness, yet no longer is it possible to change anything about it; it is too late; or else you were yourself only the instrument of suffering. . . . About that, one can do nothing.

This despair did not last long. Neither Maman nor I could have endured it longer . . . nor Alicia herself. It was killing her, as it were, before our very eyes.

For one sole instant, then, we were ourselves within Alicia, and she herself was within us, and we were upon one single shore, close enough to touch, to see one another. . . . Then despair took Alicia away . . . She began to draw off; and, abruptly, a darksome, invisible stream dug its way between us. Alicia, on the far shore, was moving away . . . mysteriously . . . she withdrew. I yearned to call her, so far gone was she already. And she, like someone about to disappear – she raised her hand and waved it toward us.

After this she seemed like a well-behaved little girl of about my age who toys with her fingers, crossing and then uncrossing them.

She died a few months later. *They* buried her, as one buries everybody, whether a person has died on the day of his death – or long before, because, maybe, of life itself. . . . What difference can there be here? . . . And why did they say of Alicia that God . . . when He came to take her . . . had shown her a mercy? . . .

# MY AUNT THÉRÉSINA VEILLEUX

My aunt Thérésina Veilleux was born in our cold province of Manitoba, and to her it was a misfortune. She suffered from asthma, and the wind that blows in our parts was one of the most malign for her; the very air harmed her . . . except when it was gentle and scented by the wild rose, as happens in the month of June. Then my aunt could breathe without too much fear.

She spent her youth reading love stories. Given the bent later assumed by her character, I think she might have preferred to read other things, but she had no choice; in the countryside where she dwelt, there then circulated only popular almanacs, or papers containing serial stories, to which a few simple souls subscribed and which were passed on from hand to hand. My aunt Thérésina read hundreds of them, even though she complained at seeing them end in so improbable a manner, poor and unlikely young girls always on the last page achieving the hand of some Hungarian or Serbian prince.

A few years later, when my aunt had children, she gave them names as uncommon among us as Serge, Maxence, Clarisse, Léopold . . . and we guessed that she had remembered them from her reading during her days as a shut-in. However that may be, my aunt was proud to have found for her children names that one certainly did not encounter frequently along our Manitoba dirt roads; and at least there was that much romance in her life.

At the period when she was reading her novelettes, nothing could have led a person to foresee that one day she would marry. "Poor Thérésina! Whoever would have her with her asthma?" people said of her, half regretfully, while pointing out that she was still young.

She had been unable to go to school – a little school between the wheat fields, two miles from her home – except for a day or two now and then; and even during the mildest seasons of the year, it happens that a shower will break or a harsh wind blow up . . . so it was often necessary for someone to undertake to see safely back home this sick child, whom they propped up in a miniature carriage drawn by a good old collie, long Thérésina's best friend.

At twenty she sometimes went to evening parties, when they were held in houses very warmly heated and tight-walled; while the others danced the polka or sang their lungs out, my aunt Thérésina remained seated, a mauve shawl around her shoulders, from time to time touching her lips with a lawn handkerchief. Thus did my uncle Majorique see her, and he loved her at once – my aunt Thérésina – beyond any possibility of change of heart. It seems that she then had very beautiful blue eyes, perhaps made brilliant by illness. Indeed, between attacks, above all when she had none for a whole week, Thérésina acquired a lively expression, pleasing and a trifle sly, as though she were more observant than the others, and my uncle Majorique, thinking that this young girl must be intelligent, liked her thus. It was long said that he saw in her a resemblance to Emily Brontë, of whom, wholly by accident, he had chanced to see a photograph; yet his imagination must have led my uncle a bit astray, for if Thérésina had a rather long face and Emily's high forehead, her eyes were wholly innocent of any of that fullness of passion immured alive.

All the same, within our family, we had warned my uncle against marriage to this young woman. "Majorique, have you given a thought to the sort of life it would involve?"

He married her during one of the hottest months in the year, so that Thérésina was able to go to the church in muslin, without a coat, having even for that day forsworn her pretty shawl of soft wool. But later on, when Thérésina's children came into the world, I remember having heard whispers and sighs, having detected looks of consternation; I remember an atmosphere of reproach, as though, each time my aunt gave birth to a child, it amounted to a real misfortune. Then, too, I was much astonished in those days that, too ill to care for her children herself, my aunt was not ill enough to avoid passing most of her time bringing them into the world. But at my age then, could anyone understand that life is furiously concerned to propagate itself, even under the most painful circumstances? And indeed, at a later age, does one understand much better?

II

After eight years, they came to settle in our city, or rather right next to us in Winnipeg. My uncle claimed that the winter must be easier to endure in a city like Winnipeg, with its streets laid out in ranks, than in regions where the farms are at least a mile apart. He likewise thought he would find in town doctors who might try something more for Thérésina than old tags of advice: always keep dry and warm, avoid rain. . . .

Having sold his farm, my uncle went into watch and clock repairing in Winnipeg. When anyone manifested a certain astonishment at his choice of this trade, my uncle laughed a little and said that we were still far indeed from conceiving all the things he knew how to do and could undertake. He explained that the city was short precisely of such repairmen; he had noticed it the very first day, as he wandered about the streets, and he had reached the conclusion that he would earn a very good living at putting clocks and watches in order. In our neighborhood, he hinted, there must be many timepieces in bad shape; they would not agree, and how many appointments that must make people miss! Beneath his joking exterior, my uncle was a man whom you eventually discovered to be full of common sense. And, in fact, he became quite skillful at his new trade.

Unfortunately, my aunt was not helped by this move made in her behalf. I recall how, when we went to see her of a January evening, we had to hasten to close behind us the heavy storm door, and then the inside door with its felt weatherstrip. Sometimes, even, thanks to excess of quickness, we caught the tails of our coats in this door. And then a straw mat must at once be thrust over the crack of the threshold. . . . Yet however speedily we observed these regulations, a bit of glacial night must have slipped into the house and reached the tiny sealed room at the end of a hallway, where my aunt kept herself snug, for very often the moment we came in, what we heard was Thérésina's gasping, terrible cough.

You did not go visit her in clothing that might still exhale something of the snow and frost; first of all you warmed yourself in front of the big stove always stuffed with logs and purring evenly; there my uncle, who never lost his gaiety, would tell us about the amusing clients he received in his Main Street shop, and he would make us laugh.

When, later on, you presented yourself before my aunt Thérésina, it did not mean that you saw her face. My aunt was still fearful of the cold air through which we had come, and of which some whiff might remain upon us, in our hair, upon our outer skins. For a year or two she had been living hooded and muffled, wrapped in a complex of blankets, and deep in a horrible sweet and sickish haze, for the Winnipeg doctors made my aunt smoke medicated cigarettes. A shawl thrown over her head, the edge of which she occasionally raised to peer at us, sheltered her like a tent; in its depths you could make out something that shone – probably Thérésina's eyes, the blue eyes my uncle Majorique had loved. A long thin hand hid the rest of the face. My aunt now breathed only from behind her hand, as though not to inhale the least bit more air than was absolutely needed. Never have I seen a person breathe with such care, prudence, and even terror.

We children, having greeted my aunt, always hastened to return to my uncle, who would sing us something or suggest a game of dominoes. To us it seemed impossible that to this huge package of skirts and wool and shawls which was my aunt you might talk, recount your enthusiasms, smile; that toward her you might become affectionate and trusting. My mother, however, carried on real conversations with the odd bundle seated on the edge of the bed, and she must even have inspired it to laughter, for at times the whole mass of blankets would shake in a motion at once funny and frightening. But soon a wheezing would emerge from it, the motion would change aspect, and everyone would rush to help my aunt regain her breath, gently tap her back, hold her up, try to forestall an attack. In fact, laughing was even more baneful to my aunt than breathing. And hence not often were amusing or witty things recounted to my aunt Thérésina. Moreover, even on such occasions, she showed preference for people with afflictions . . . and in this department my mother spoiled her, telling her for a whole evening long about a veritable crowd of wretched beings who aroused my aunt's interest. She would nod and conclude, "Yes, indeed! There are those worse off than we!"

Meanwhile, my mother always claimed that during those long winter nights she herself learned a great deal from my aunt, for if Thérésina was incapable of sewing or cooking herself, she knew very well how one must go about it to succeed in all things. Remote from any practical knowledge, she had accumulated very sound theories about everything – a trifle harsh and authoritarian, but most sound, Maman insisted. Then, too, having a great deal of time to watch people make mistakes, commit serious blunders, my aunt had acquired a remarkable capacity for criticism; she could put her finger on exactly the spot where others went wrong. It was even a truly extraordinary thing that, never venturing forth, living immured and beyond movement, she should have been able to run her house very efficiently, know everything that went on, not only in her own home, but in almost every part of the city. She was the first to inform my mother of the behavior of our cousin Yvonne – her parents had entrusted her to mine so that she might finish her schooling in our city – our cousin Yvonne, whom we thought very devout, since every evening she went to church, but who, in fact, used this as a cover for her meetings with a certain Monsieur Belleau, a newcomer, especially worrisome because no one knew anything about his antecedents. And this time my mother was truly incensed – more against Thérésina, indeed, than against Yvonne.

But my aunt Thérésina's real passion, far more than for criticism, was, above all else, for geraniums. She had some of a shade of red so unsullied, so bright, that I have never seen the like since. When she was not too indisposed, my aunt would come look at them in the small pots lined up along her windows. She would dust them – I can still see the way she did it! – with the tip of her finger, delicately cleaning off their leaves, and she would say. "You must not leave dust on the leaves of plants; plants breathe through their leaves; plants need good air." And she was still overjoyed to be alive when the month of June came round and she could set her geraniums out in the open. My uncle would offer to do this task for her. He pointed out to her that by going close to the still damp, cool soil, she would lay herself open to aggravating her malady. But, protected by three or four sweaters, a small trowel in her hand, one fine day my aunt would herself emerge to set out her plants.

Alas, the Manitoba summer is very short. With the first autumn rains, Thérésina had to return to her tiny overheated room, reeking with the smell of the dreadful cigarettes which she began once more to smoke. And my uncle Majorique would begin to say that Manitoba did not in the least suit Thérésina's illness, that she needed a wholly different land . . . California, for instance . . . yes, why not California?

"She, who so loves plants," my uncle would say, "does it make any sense that she can only see them and enjoy them for two months in the year? . . ." And he sent to a travel agency for pamphlets and all sorts of information about California.

Thus it was, by means of brochures and vividly colored post cards – they were thought to be overvivid – that California loomed up for us on the frozen prairie horizon, not too far off, and wonderfully real, with small white houses basking in the sun!

From this medley of cards sent to my uncle, my aunt chose one that showed geraniums – no longer mere plants, but almost trees! – covered with huge and glorious flowers. My aunt folded this bit of paper and preserved it between the pages of her prayer book, alongside pictures of the Pope and mementos of the dead bearing the words "In Memoriam." Thus, from the start, did my aunt show sympathy for California.

She would look at the little white stucco houses on the post cards and would say, "See! They're pretty as places to live!"

She already knew that inside these small dwellings there is a garden which is called a "patio."

And finally she invited my mother to come visit her someday in California.

"When we get there," explained my aunt, "you'll come, Eveline. I'll make you come. You, with your rheumatism – it will do you good, too!"

In our family all of us were far from taking too seriously my uncle's new idea. We spoke of it as a silly scheme. Silly? . . . Yes . . . certainly . . . if you thought of the distance, of the money required. All the same, my uncle had looked into the matter seriously: the American government would allow him to establish himself with his family in the United States, but in view of the fact that my aunt was incurable, only on condition of his possessing a capital sum of ten thousand dollars. Apart from that, as far as the warmer air and sunlight were concerned, wasn't the plan the most reasonable thing in the world? Of course, my uncle was far from possessing the capital required by the government of the United States.

So, for want of anything better, and since he had heard that the Saskatchewan climate was auspicious for bronchial infections, my uncle left our city and took all his family to live in Gravelbourg.

III

In Saskatchewan, not only does it blow in winter, but almost all summer, and perhaps the summer wind there is more noxious than the winter. We used to be told – we who had never seen the desert, nor a great deal of Saskatchewan – that the wind blowing there felt as though it came off the Sahara. Yet, through such comparisons, our imaginations heard from afar the Gravelbourg wind, that sad, hot, desiccating wind; all day it sucked up the poor soil, reducing it to wandering, miserable dust. Thus, particle by particle, the best of the land disappeared. My aunt Thérésina wrote us a short and very sad letter, in which she said, "Dear Eveline: I take my pen in hand to tell you that here all goes well enough, except that I cannot go out, even in midsummer. The wind chokes me . . . the cattle perish . . . the wells are drying up. . . ."

Out there my uncle had found too much competition in his trade as watch repairer – or rather, better opportunities for prosperity in another. He became a lumber merchant; in those days a new house was being completed in Gravelbourg every week. The first year he sold I know not how many thousands of board feet. Nevertheless, since the climate was not exactly what suited Thérésina, my uncle was already seeking a buyer for all the wood remaining on his hands. My aunt drew on her reserves of patience. She retained her faith in the California plan, and henceforth ended her letters with such phrases as: "We have got a little closer, it's true, to California, but not so much so, when you think it over. . . . It must come soon, because, before long, I shan't even have the strength to leave this dreadful Gravelbourg. . . ."

Then we learned that my uncle Majorique, after four and one half years spent at Gravelbourg, had turned even farther west. The family had made its move; the letter bearing us the news was posted from North Battleford.

Whatever could have induced my uncle to select this town? Gravelbourg might do in a pinch! It was a French Canadian center relatively toward the south, and when the family arrived there, they had run into a few acquaintances; but North Battleford! That ugly pioneer town established in mud, at the moment resounding from dawn to dusk with the racket of hammers, passing through a turbulent boom, like the towns of the Klondike during the gold rush! We have long thought that my uncle's sole motive for deciding upon this stop along his way was to acquire some money there. He was able to revert to his former trade, to which he added that of jeweler. "Two things that go together," wrote my uncle, "for here there are many rich, and I feel I can sell them without trouble small diamonds for engagement rings and other odds and ends of precious stones – not too costly – for anniversaries . . ."

At about this time, however, while my uncle was going full steam ahead, my aunt began to withdraw her confidence. She would henceforth refer to him as "the Utopian!" or "the Dreamer!" and things even less flattering. "You know your brother," she wrote to Maman, "full of wild fancies and un-stable! . . . I go bouncing from town to town; scarcely have we time to unpack our things when our fine Majorique wants to move again. . . . California! Yes! Talk about California! At the rate we're going, one of these days we'll end up in Alaska!

When you get right down to it, I wonder whether your brother hasn't made an excuse out of this California scheme to satisfy his fidgets. . . ."

For his own part, my uncle Majorique complained to us a little about my aunt Thérésina. "The poor woman is becoming quite ill tempered. I know it is her dreadful illness that makes her this way, and I myself don't mind too much . . . but the children are growing up . . . and they don't like to be scolded all the time. I'm afraid we shall not keep Maxence and Clarisse at home with us much longer."

Obviously to my aunt Thérésina, cheerfulness, bustle, songs, dancing – all such things seemed less and less natural. We heard that she was strict with her daughters and her grown sons. However, what she deplored the most was that Serge had retraced his steps to Gravelbourg, where he was managing the lumber business. Then she had Clarisse to regret; she had found a match – a wealthy one, according to my uncle – at North Battleford.

"We leave children in every town through which we pass," my aunt wrote; "we soon shall not have a single one left . . . what a diaspora!" And she reverted, making it responsible for all these misfortunes, to that stupid scheme of going to California. "We should indeed have stayed home," she told us. And now there could be no vestige of doubt that, through time's weird alchemy – that transformation in our memories which it alone is capable of effecting – the years spent in Manitoba, and even the stifling little Winnipeg room, had become for my aunt the best part of her life.

It was sixteen years after they had left us that we learned they had reached Edmonton.

"Good Lord!" exclaimed my mother. "Think of choosing Edmonton! The northernmost city in Canada! Poor Thérésina, she's good and far from California now!" Suffering more and more from rheumatism, my mother had reached the point of wishing as much for herself as for my aunt that she might see them at last settled in California, since the invitation to pay them a visit there in orange blossom time had never been withdrawn. And nothing seemed more surprising to me in those days than this eagerness to get away manifested by the older people among us. Just the opposite of what happens elsewhere, where it is the young who want to journey forth, here it was the poor souls weary of the cold, the sick, the arthritic, all those who were beset with age or feeling poorly. Why, we young people were keen about the tingling winter, the snow crunching under our feet, our breath freezing as it left our lips, the droll fringes of frost over our lashes, and, overhead, the blue sheen of the stars, as well as, on occasion, the great far-flung play of the aurora borealis!

From Edmonton we received only one single brief letter from Thérésina, which began saying, "I take my pen in hand to tell you that today the thermometer registers fifty-five below zero. . . . Even the horses can't go out. I thought I used to know what cold is like; my mistake was to have complained of it too soon. . . ." Toward the end she told us: "That fine fellow Majorique finds Edmonton a city of the future. . . . He speaks of the future as though we were still twenty years old. . . . As for me, I must be drawing near my end. . . . It was not God's will that I go down into the South. God's will be done."

Later on she was too wretched to give us news. We heard of them through Noémi, who became a trained nurse, settled in Edmonton, and refused to leave when the rest of the family moved on toward Vancouver.

My aunt had become so pessimistic, so thoroughly certain that she would go forever from cold to colder, that in British Columbia she long refused to believe the air was soft and agreeable. One day, however, having taken a few steps out of doors, my aunt, who believed that she was still living in a region where nature was cruel, saw roses in bloom. She sent us some of their dried petals, telling my mother, "Maybe you won't believe it – I picked them on the twenty-eighth of February, while I thought of you, my dear Eveline. . . ." A little joy, we saw with pleasure, was rebuilding feelings of affection in our poor aunt's heart.

But the coastal fogs did her asthma no good. Eventually my aunt shut herself up out there in a stifling little room, as she had done almost all her life, be it here or be it there, and when you came down to it, as she said – how much had she seen of so many cities, of the many weary miles she had traveled, of the almost entire continent she had traversed?

At that juncture my uncle was setting up a laundry business. Ever young, alert, and enterprising, he had certainly just discovered that in this city there were too few laundrymen. This undertaking flourished so mightily that within two or three years he had a string of branch stores and his third son, Léopold, could take over its management. This son of his was to remain in Vancouver; and so, even today, almost all across the country there are children of my aunt Thérésina and my uncle Majorique, as though to prove once and for all that these constant moves, their unbelievable wanderings, were no mere figment of the imagination. As for my uncle, at last we realized to how great an extent, despite all appearances, he had been a man of one set idea . . . that if he had taken a northern route to go south and then had veered west, he had all the same been making his way toward his goal. In any case, relying upon the good faith of a real-estate agent, he bought a parcel of land in California. It was said that he arranged the purchase before leaving in order the better to make up my aunt's mind, for had the money not been invested and the place ready to receive Thérésina, almost certainly she would have been unwilling, despite the fog, to set off once more.

It lay very close to a small village called Buena Vista or Bella Vista. The property included an orchard containing principally orange and avocado trees. A little withdrawn from the coast, it had a view over the ocean, and one could also glimpse, but very far off, mountains covered with snow. A small house stood waiting for my uncle and aunt. The garden was completely sheltered from the wind, with exposure to the best sunshine of the day. For the moment, however, the most distressing question was whether my aunt Thérésina would be able to stand the trip. Her heart was much weakened. And that winter the rest of us back in Manitoba would ask ourselves, from day to day, "Is Thérésina ever going to arrive in California?"

"Often," my mother would say, "it is at the very moment when one's lifetime desire lies within reach that it is suddenly snatched away!"

IV

She got there, but shaken by the trip, stubborn, already old – true enough – and she refused, as it were, to believe she was there. None the less, she at last began to shed her sweaters, her heavy quilted and interlined skirts, her headband, an old gray muffler that had traveled with her from Manitoba.

And her last and dear child, Rachel, whom we had never seen, wrote us: "We had believed – we had all believed – that Maman was a fairly stout person, on the well-rounded side, eh! Well! When we had taken off the flannel garments which she wore over very nearly all parts of her body, the knitted clothing, and then still more layers of flannel and knit goods, oh, Aunt Eveline! We then realized that of Maman herself there remained almost nothing! . . ."

But, without letting on too much, they watched how this tiny old woman would react when she saw a nature, a country, a sky that would not be hostile to her, that – quite the opposite – had been made to her order. My uncle, Rachel, Roberto, all were eager to see my aunt's face when she really became aware of God's creation. But they gave no hint of it: my aunt was put out of sorts whenever anyone noticed the brief moments during which she was still a little joyful.

The day came at last when my aunt dared venture into the open air with her hands and face uncovered.

And if the tiny kingdom of God then before her eyes in the least resembled the post card view of it that we received, it must be granted that it was a fine summary of what God could create when His preoccupation was to rejoice the eyes of men.

To the left there was a path bordered with eucalyptus, and the air was made wholly pure by their big, disheveled leaves. On the other side there were bushy rhododendrons and poinsettias. And then, beyond other masses of plants, far away, my aunt surely could glimpse the sea. They told her that this was the Pacific Ocean, that here it deserved its name, and that its langorous waves washed up on the beaches shells from distant isles, perhaps from Hawaii. They led my aunt toward a garden chair so placed that Thérésina could see the valley and water merely by moving her eyes a little. Above her armchair waved syringa branches in bloom.

Two or three times she came back to sit beneath the

syringas. They found her there one day, her eyes wide open and staring fixedly forever. And in Thérésina's blue eyes, there was a deep questioning, as though in leaving this world my poor aunt's soul had asked itself, "Why? But why?"

About the meaning of this "why," though, we never agreed in our family. Some claimed that my aunt must have asked God why she should die now that she had arrived; others felt that, looking at the snowy mountains, it was Manitoba that she saw once again, loved and sorrowed for, perhaps, as always; and thus that she had asked herself why she was here, and not there, in her own land, to die.

There cannot exist a better place to abide in than the tiny cemetery attached to the old Spanish mission of San Juan Capistrano. A wind as light as a child's breath stirs a little the wild leaves of the eucalyptus. The pepper trees trail, delicate as the shroud covering the body of a dead young girl, their long, fine foliage. Of no great height, and the color of Mexican pottery jars, a wall of baked earth surrounds this garden; this primitive masonry is called "adobe"; transpose two of its letters and you get "abode," a dwelling place. And here indeed is the habitation of thousands of swallows.

Every year, on the seventeenth of March exactly, and at a set hour as well, they arrive there. Spectators who have taken their places near at hand somewhat ahead of time, await the squadron. At the appointed hour, the sky darkens toward the sea; the whirlwind of birds takes shape, and, on the dot, the swallows dive into their home in the cemetery.

But when my aunt died, there had long been no free space in the San Juan Capistrano cemetery.

My uncle offered a large sum to the prior, yet he refused all the same. Every inch of this garden had been taken for many years, said he; moreover, the famous enclosure, said he, was in the process of becoming a sort of museum.

Then patiently, maybe with a few tears – he imagined that he had caused his wife's death by dragging her to California – my uncle briefly told Thérésina's strange story; how she was born in one of Canada's coldest provinces; how, as a little girl she had never been able to go to school more than a few days at a time, even though she would have liked to acquire book learning; how, at parties during her youth, she could not dance, which later on had made dancing seem to her frivolous and reprehensible; in short, my uncle pleaded so well that the prior of San Juan Capistrano grew perplexed. While gently moving the branch of a pepper tree, he seemed to be considering the extraordinary destiny of my aunt, born Thérésina Veilleux, and even the coldness there had been all through that life! . . .

Then he hinted that perhaps . . . perhaps they might dig a grave above another very ancient one; there were some dating back to Spanish days, two hundred years before – maybe even longer – thus, the prior was saying, the family of this dead person, most likely extinct, could not take offense, or the dead person either, reduced as he was to a few dry bits of bone. . . . He himself, the prior, in his white robes, seemed to imagine very well that for this dead Manitoba woman there could exist no better burial than within these walls so long baked by the sun.

And this is why, over the grave of my aunt Thérésina Veilleux, all day long the birds sing.

# L'ITALIENNE

At the time, we had on top of our Bell piano, amidst photographs of Georgianna, of Gervais as an academy student, of myself, and I know not what other pictures, but long since in the position of honor, a sort of blue pitcher with two handles and a long neck – a flower vase, I imagine, but in which we no longer put anything, to spare the poor relic, which was badly battered. Its varnish was scaling; the chipped top of the vase revealed the white, friable material – probably plaster – of which it was made. I loathed it and dusted it without giving it much heed; one day I chipped it even more by knocking it over on the piano. Maman came rushing to see what had happened. She looked at me almost angrily.

"Butter fingers!" she cried. "Can't you be careful of my Milan jug?"

I was about to answer when I realized that Maman's anger, assuredly like many people's, was no more than wearisome regret, the accumulation of many hurts in her heart. And then I recalled how the Milan jug had come into our home. . . .

In those days I was still a very small girl; it was before Alicia's death; it must even have been before Odette said good-by to the world. Every month my father would proudly bring us what we needed to live . . . and to indulge a few notions as well. I think that we were very happy, since we had only the most ordinary worries: thus, would the fine empty fields west of our house remain so? One day or another should we not see rising there some wretched structure which would cut off our view and shut out our lovely early sunlight? Up until then it invaded unhindered all our windows on that side, and there were several of them that faced east; in those days care was taken to face the windows of a house toward the warmest sun of the day. Yes, I believe this was then our most serious worry: would we lose our sunshine!

But for the time being few people were tempted to come live in our section; it had its back toward town; its face, as it were, turned toward the fields . . . and those empty fields near us remained open to our uses. Papa had obtained from the city hall permission to make a vegetable garden there. Farther on there was a space to play at Sioux Indians and ambushes; and beyond there was even more room, which Monsieur Gauthier, our neighbor to the east and a marble worker, employed for his own purposes: for months on end he would leave lying there cruciform stones, which the wild hay would finally half conceal, or at times cherubs and monuments of Manitoba stone, the extraordinarily pure white Tyndale stone. In sum, to the east of us there was a stretch of tilled soil, then an area of brush where stood our small children's tents made of burlap bags, and, a trifle farther, a gentle cemetery without any dead. A few of the headstones, unfinished or perhaps spoiled by Monsieur Gauthier, remained there indefinitely, their epitaphs hanging in suspense: To the pious memory of . . . good wife . . . good mother. . . . On some of them you could still decipher, upon the darkened face of the stone: Deceased at the age of twenty-two years, three months, fourteen days. Was it not odd? In those times they calculated to within a single day the span of human life!

But one evening Papa came home full of excitement, bringing us overwhelming news. "Just guess," said he gloomily to my mother.

Maman could not guess.

"The lot next to us is sold," said Papa.

And, what was worse, someone was going to build a house there. The buyer, Papa said, was an Italian, newly come to this country.

"An Italian!" cried Maman. "As long as he's no Sicilian bandit!"

The very next day, scarcely giving us time to get used to the catastrophe, men came to dig a cellar in this soil next to ours and, for our taste, too close to our house. Still, the cellar's dimensions were restrained; the house that was to rise there perhaps would not greatly cut off our sun.

We were not yet entirely reassured when there stepped off the tram linking us to Winnipeg a broad, tall man with dead-black hair, his eyes likewise black and shining, sporting a black mustache with twisted ends, a large man in blue work clothes and a broad straw hat, who came to begin building all by himself the house next door. Lumber had been delivered; in a twinkling the man with the mustache had laid out a dozen planks and begun nailing them together, meanwhile striking up a song in Italian; Maman said it must be something from an opera. During a pause in the singing, Maman spoke to him from our porch; she learned that his name was Giuseppe Sariano, that he was a carpenter by trade, and that this time he was working as his own boss; yes, it was his own home he was putting up. Then we heard him singing louder than ever.

Thereupon Maman asserted that he seemed a fine man, and she persuaded my father to "sound out" the Italian.

"Above all, try to discover," Maman urged him, "whether he intends to build as high as we."

My father talked for quite a time with the Italian, who could not reply to the least question without jumping from one foot to the other, turning now east, now west, and agitating his entire body. Papa came back, and by his pace we could see that the news was good. And in fact, Papa was laughing to himself; he did not laugh much in his life, but that day his shoulders shook a little as he hastened to bring back to us what the Italian had said.

At first, Papa having asked him, "Do you intend to build a large house? . . ." the Italian had jumped up and down and announced: "*Si . . . si . . .* very fine . . . very big house!" . . . "As large as mine?" The Italian had looked appalled. "Oh no! Oh, la, la! Not a castle; I have a very small wife, not very strong, tiny, tiny. She would be lost in your *château*. . . . And then my small wife would die keeping up, cleaning so large a place. But all the same I'm building big!" Overjoyed at Papa's interest, the Italian had pulled out of his pocket the design he himself had made for his home.

Recollecting it, Papa was again seized by a gentle gaiety.

"Have you any idea," he asked Maman, "how big this house will be? About the size of our kitchen, as nearly as I could judge. . . . No, come to think of it, I imagine one could fit two of them into our kitchen. . . ."

"Probably in Italy," Maman remarked, "that would pass for a large house."

It turned out in fact to be a humble and pleasant wooden

bungalow, without any upper floor, and we enjoyed watching it take shape, since it would never hide from us our view or our sunlight.

Was it then, or a little later, and because he did us no harm, that all of us together took to liking the Italian?

In any case, from the very first day, and on all the days that followed, I spent almost all my time watching him work, through a chink in our board fence; and at home no one seemed annoyed at my almost incessant reports. Indeed, up to that point our sympathy for this man was based upon very little: he was erecting a small house, he had a tiny, tiny wife who soon would be leaving Milan and would arrive when the house was completed; moreover, he sang operas. Papa, however, must have thought that this was sufficient to justify friendship, for suddenly he informed Maman: "Suppose I gave him the plum tree!"

This was a fine small tree the roots of which were in our land, but which bore its branches, its fruit, and all its upper trunk on the other side of our fence and hence over the Italian's property. And Papa did as he had said he would: he went in person to present the tree to the Italian.

On the porch Maman waited to learn how the Italian would receive the gift. And Papa reported that the Italian must be sentimental after the Italian fashion; the moment he knew the tree was his, he had fingered it, stroked its bark; he had even kissed it, saying, "I am owner of a tree! No sooner do I set foot in Canada, you may say, than I get a tree – full grown and bearing fruit! Heaven is with Giuseppe Sariano." That was the way with Italians, said Papa; they bubbled over for no good reason; they overdid things.

Did this effervescence of our neighbor win us completely? Did it set the example? Maman began to wonder whether he had brought anything to eat with him, whether it would not be appropriate to send him some hot soup. . . . I would go flatten myself against the hole in the fence; then I would come back to inform that others that the Italian had his food in a small tin box, that at this very moment, his back against our wooden fence, he was eating bread and raw onions and drinking a red liquid straight from a bottle. Once I had passed on the news, I returned to keep an eye on our man. As far as I could make out, he was rather badly shaved; not only his beard and his skin were dark, but also the tiny hairs he had in his ears and nostrils. For my inspection I had a quite adequate hole in one of the boards; as for him, I don't think he was able to see me – at most my eye glued to this opening in the fence. Right now he was asleep, stretched out on the grass, his straw hat over his nose. From the edges of his lips, shaped in something like a pout, slight sounds emerged. A bit of straw must have been tickling him somewhere; from time to time he made an effort to turn over, but he was too sound asleep to succeed, and each time he fell back with his belly upmost. I wondered what I might do to increase the well-being of so nice a man from Italy. Papa did not seem to me to have been generous enough, for, after all, the plum tree did not have to be given; it was already there, leaning over the Italian's land. I was determined to offer far more. And then I thought of Papa's small strawberry bed.

Few people in our city, and most likely in all Manitoba, had succeeded in growing any as plump or as sweet. Yet alas! Papa knew each of his strawberries individually: two fine ones, red all over and almost at the point of perfection, another still white on the face away from the sun, five or six more not nearly ready to eat. There was no way to filch any of them without his noticing it. Not that Papa was stingy with his strawberries. He merely liked to reserve for himself the pleasure of one fine day bringing us a small cup filled with them, which he would place on the table, remarking with false modesty, "There are really not enough of them to be worthwhile, just sufficient to give you a taste!"

So that day, that I, also, might give pleasure, I shattered discipline. I went and chose the two large strawberries which were at their best, and then for good measure – because two would not do without a third! – I plucked the fruit that was a trifle white on one side. It was munificent! Three strawberries for one single person! Never had I purloined more than one at a time for myself. But our Italian was so large a man! I moved toward him, my three strawberries in the fold of my turned-up dress.

He was still asleep, and his open mouth emitted blasts of air which bent the hair overhanging his forehead. I put one berry in his mouth, then another, whereupon his Adam's apple gave an alarming jerk; perhaps he was beginning to taste the fruit, or else he had almost choked. Be this as it may, since his mouth remained open, I hastily shoved into it the third berry. This, however, was the least ripe; I should certainly have begun with it and finished with the best.

The Italian wakened completely. He yawned a little, beating the air with his arms. I was crouching in the grass, examining him from close by. When he opened his eyes, he saw mine watching him. At the same instant he surely must have tasted the last strawberry I had just slipped into his mouth. The other two, sadly enough, must have gone straight down; but this one he seemed to recognize for what it was. He sat up in the grass, laughing and stretching his arms a little. And he said, as though it were my name, "Strawberry! Little Strawberry! Charming little Strawberry!"

I instantly liked being called Strawberry, perhaps because I so little resembled one, with my ever-drawn, pale small face, the circles round my eyes, my barked knees. Petite Misère suited me better. But how I liked this other name, as though I were good to eat! Then I asked the Italian, "Are you a Sicilian bandit?"

"*Banditto!*"

He roared with laughter; his belly – broad and full – shook. Whereupon, in the grass, he drew me into his arms – Papa was right in saying that Italians have a sentimental nature – and he told me that his poor, tiny wife, always ailing, could not have children, that perhaps he would never have a little daughter. . . . And with this he began to kiss me.

I did not know exactly how to confess to the theft of the three strawberries; I returned home rather sheepish and began by admitting, "The Italian kissed me."

Papa and Maman exchanged one of those looks; I mean by "one of those looks" the sort that seem to be signals between grownups. Papa got up, slightly clenching his fists.

"What's that you say?" Maman asked me.

Papa grumbled, "One's always in a hurry to make friends with foreigners!"

Then Maman spoke to me briefly about men: she told me that little girls should not let themselves be kissed by them, except on very special occasions – some extraordinary joy or emotion.

I told her that that was exactly what it had been – a fit of emotion.

All the same, they repeated that I must watch my step. I asked myself what step. The next day, though, the Italian told Papa the tale of the three strawberries; Papa in his turn told my mother, who repeated it to the neighbors . . . and steps no longer needed watching, which suited me. I have always liked to be close to someone who is at work; even as a very small child I preferred to watch someone working rather than play myself, and how fast and well the Italian worked. In short order the frame of the little bungalow was up. But we still chatted on, the Italian and I, he from above, his legs hanging down, nails clamped in the corner of his mouth; I from below, my head lifted toward the sun, and shading my eyes with my hand. And sometimes up there the Italian would commence a great "a-a-a-a" of song – the beginning of one of his opera arias. Maman would come out on our porch the better to hear the singing. She said of the Italian, "His heart is on his sleeve." She would make a trumpet of her hands, so that her voice might carry to our neighbor, and she would ask through this trumpet, "Have you any more news of Madame Sariano?" The Italian would tumble down, search his pockets, extract, all rumpled up, the last letter from Italy. He would read it to Maman: "I shall soon take to the seas, once more to meet my Giuseppe; I count the days, the hours. . . . Give my greetings to those good Canadian neighbors of whom you speak in your last letter . . . to the little Strawberry. . . ."

Having read the letter, Giuseppe would clamber back again to his hammering, making up for lost time.

"Have you ever seen a happier man!" Maman would exclaim.

She said it with a noble envy, neither sad nor malicious, the sort of envy you never feel for wealth or prestige – with an envy springing from the heart.

The bungalow was finished; now the Italian was furnishing it, and regarding every detail he would come ask Maman's advice. Where was it best to place the stove? Maman urged him, since his wife was small, to remember to keep the cupboards within her reach. And, indeed, had it not been for Maman, Giuseppe would have put them far too high.

At last the Italian woman must have arrived and been installed in their bungalow, but there was naught to be seen of either of them; it was as though no one dwelt in their direction, and Maman forbade me to go there, saying that both of them certainly were eager to be left to themselves for some time. But the Italian could not have been of this opinion; the next morning he came very early, calling out to us, "Are you all dead?" It was to introduce us to Lisa, hidden behind the breadth of her husband's back, whom he was gently leading by the hand.

II

She was even thinner and smaller-boned than we had thought from the photographs Giuseppe had shown us. She spoke in a soft, very weak voice; it was like a murmur. And Maman explained, "It's because of her Italian accent. The Italian tongue is extremely musical."

But, although embarrassed, she had her manners, and you became aware of it once she had a trifle conquered her timidity and also, of course, the amazement she felt at suddenly finding herself on Rue Deschambault.

Giuseppe had daily to travel considerable distances to build houses; but before he began, he came to ask Maman whether she would try to distract Lisa a trifle. He pointed out what had already occurred to us: how far it was from Milan to the brand-new bungalow; so could Maman help Lisa to overcome her loneliness? Maman promised to do her best.

Every morning from then on Giuseppe left our street at an early hour. He would emerge accompanied by Lisa. She walked a little way with him; then he kissed her, strode on a bit, turned around again to look at her. Then he would almost always have to run to catch the tram, which was waiting, its step lowered and ready . . . True enough, the conductor never hurried these final farewells by clanging his bell.

At evening it was even more affecting. A streetcar would halt. We saw the Italian getting off, covered with sawdust and bits of wood. His pace was that of a tired man. His body leaned forward; his toolbox looked heavy to carry. Yet soon, when he beheld the windows of his bungalow, he began to straighten up; he smoothed his mustache. Then Lisa came out and started off to meet him. Giuseppe also quickened his pace. He dropped his toolbox and lifted his wife off the ground; he would hoist her up, taking all of her in his great arms. And while he held her thus, you could see Lisa's feet, free of the ground, kicking the empty air.

Maman would be standing behind a curtain, which she raised cautiously the better to see them embrace. Then she let the curtain fall back and said, with joy, with envy, "How much he loves her!"

And sometimes she would add, "A woman's finest crown is to be loved. There is nothing – no topaz, nor diamond, nor amethyst, nor emerald, nor ruby that can better bring out a woman's beauty!"

Yet Giuseppe's little Italian wife seemed to me awfully frail and skinny! For my own part, I often went to call upon her. These were real visits, for the Italian woman received me exactly as one grownup receives another. She made me sit down in her living room, and she sat facing me. Nor did her feet quite reach the floor. She would ask me, "How is Madame your mother? Monsieur your father?" I would politely reply, "Very well, thank you." Then I, in my turn, would ask, "How is Monsieur your husband? . . ." I was delighted with these conversations patterned on those I had with other little girls when we played at being grown ladies.

Later I learned that, to please her husband, Lisa was learning French from a book replete with exactly the sort of phrases she addressed to me. No matter! She uttered them with all the requisite feeling. But I did not yet understand how she was better adorned than with rubies, emeralds, and topazes. Moreover, not one of us, not even Maman, who so frequently alluded to them, had ever seen any such stones. What on earth was love, to be better still? "Your father," Maman would say, "also loves you; see all the sacrifices he makes for you!" Yes, surely Papa was filled with love, and to the point that it constantly made him suffer, was an almost eternal torment. The Italian carried his love upon his countenance, like a sun. But this was past our envy; it was doubtless unattainable, presumably a product of Italy, as Maman herself granted. "Such a love, I can tell you, is not to seen every day. Is there anything rarer?"

Yet we only loved the Italian woman the better for her being so cherished by her Giuseppe. Is that just? Is it just to love someone already so richly loved? I should have thought it more charitable to save our love for those who, having had none from the outset, would perhaps by the same token never know any.

"However, that's the way it is," Maman would say, "and we can't change it; does not all the world love a lover?"

Meanwhile, Lisa was none the better for it. Our Italian, his face now clouded, seemingly full of wrath, talked to Maman about her. "She's going; I shall lose her," he would say; "she has no more strength than a bird. . . . And loneliness is finishing her off. I thought a change of air . . . But no!" he would exclaim, thumping his sturdy chest. "I have torn her from her country . . . and it's killing her. . . ."

"Oh, not a bit of it!" Maman would console him. "She'll get over it. Don't be so hard on yourself, Giuseppe Sariano; there's no happier woman in the world than yours! . . ."

### III

Nevertheless, it was he who died, suddenly, in the full light of the sun, upon the ridgepole of a house he was building, and of an apoplectic stroke. People said that it was not surprising when you thought it over, for he was a heavy eater, a wine drinker, a man of fiery temperament, his blood too rich, too thick. . . . Such was what they said about our Italian when he was dead.

And so there remained nothing – did there? – to keep the Italian woman in our parts. She seemed smaller, more lost in Manitoba than a twelve-year-old, and she was to return to Italy, carrying with her in a casket the embalmed body of Giuseppe Sariano.

We went to pay her a visit of condolence, Maman and I. Out of respect Maman wore her heavy coat, which was black; I possessed only one dark piece of clothing, my navy-blue dress. The Italian woman seated us in her little parlor, as of old when I went there by myself in quest of news of her husband.

She stretched wide her arms to us, saying, "Dear Lady, dear Child, you were so kind to Giuseppe! . . . You whom Giuseppe loved so dearly! . . ."

Giuseppe had been noisy, demonstrative, even in sorrow; she was calm; you might have likened her to a sad, tiny brook, which wept softly as it ran. And this was good of her: gently she sought to console us for our loss of Giuseppe Sariano.

"So, then," said Maman, wiping her eyes, "it's true; we're going to lose you, too. You're returning to Italy?"

Lisa politely excused herself. "I'd like to bury Giuseppe Sariano over there . . . in the sun . . ." said she.

"Yes," said Maman, "the sun! We imagine that we know it here!"

And although it was scarcely the time to talk of it, Maman asked: "Tell me a bit more about Italy. . . . You will see it again . . . but I, shall I ever behold it?"

For this is what had happened: Maman in trying to take the Italian woman's mind off Italy had herself acquired a homesickness for that land. Still, it had been good for Lisa to watch Maman fall in love with Italy. She had shown her post cards with many Italian sights: Saint Peter's in Rome; a ceiling covered with paintings, which must be hard to look at up there above your head; a tower which leaned askew; Pompeii, where people dead for centuries had not budged an inch – there was even a chained dog amidst the ruins – and a dreadful volcano that every twenty years spewed forth lava. Maman had become interested in all these things, and especially in a wretched picture of the Milan cathedral, all pink and pale blue. Maman likewise was crazy about a kind of blue jug which the Italian woman told her she had bought from an almost blind potter on the streets of Milan. On the same occasion Lisa had recounted how the potters worked in the streets and sang over their tasks; that, wretched and poor, they were, none the less, often happier than the rich. . . . Was it because of this that Maman loved Italy? And did she love the crock for Italy's sake?

The time came for us to part. Maman, standing up, scarcely knew what to do. But the Italian woman, diminutive though she might be, knew how people say farewell.

"Take," said she to Maman, "some object here in my house, which will speak to you of myself, of my late husband. I have nothing of great value; so do take, I beg you, something which may tempt you a little. . . ."

Then I saw Maman, despite herself, glance at the jug. I longed to call her attention to a lovely sea shell, in which you could hear the roar of the ocean. But, while protesting that she couldn't make up her mind to take any of the so very pretty things there were in the parlor, Maman kept her eyes fixed on the jug.

The Italian woman took the vase, which stood on a bracket, dusted it a bit, and held it out to her.

"Oh, that's much too much!" said Maman. "I couldn't . . . I shouldn't deprive you of anything so handsome!"

"Come, now!" said the Italian woman. "I'll find a thousand like it in Milan. Please take it; you'll give me such great pleasure."

So Maman yielded to her joy; supporting the crock in her hands, she held it off a little, the better to admire it, and then clasped it to her heart like a thing of price one has lost and then found again.

We went back with our jug. So real and strong was her happiness in bringing it home that Maman seemed for a few moments forgetful of the Italian woman's impending departure.

However, on the day when the taxi came to fetch Lisa, Maman, standing on our porch, watched her go; and when, at the end of our street, the dust had settled, when there remained of it no more than a powdering, such as might have been stirred up by footsteps long since passed, Maman raised her hand toward this nebulous golden spoor and said to us, "The sun of Italy . . . today . . . leaves our street!"

# WILHELM

My first suitor came from Holland. He was called Wilhelm and his teeth were too regular; he was much older than I; he had a long, sad face . . . at least thus it was that others made me see him when they had taught me to consider his defects. As for me, at first I found his face thoughtful rather than long and peaked. I did not yet know that his teeth – so straight and even – were false. I thought I loved Wilhelm. Here was the first man who, through me, could be made happy or unhappy; here was a very serious matter.

I had met him at our friends the O'Neills', who still lived not far from us in their large gabled house on Rue Desmeurons. Wilhelm was their boarder; for life is full of strange things: thus this big, sad man was a chemist in the employ of a small paint factory then operating in our city, and – as I have said – lodged with equally uprooted people, the O'Neills, formerly of County Cork in Ireland. A far journey to have come merely to behave, in the end, like every-one else – earn your living, try to make friends, learn our lan-guage, and then, in Wilhelm's case, love someone who was not for him. Do adventures often turn out so tritely? Obviously enough, though, in those days I did not think so.

Evenings at the O'Neills' were musical. Kathleen played "Mother Machree," while her mother, seated on a sofa, wiped her eyes, trying the while to avert our attention, to direct it away from herself, for she did not like people to believe her so deeply stirred by Irish songs. Despite the music, Elizabeth kept right on digging away at her arithmetic; she still was utterly indifferent to men. But Kathleen and I cared a great deal. We feared dreadfully to be left on the shelf; we feared we should fail to be loved and to love with a great and absolutely unique passion.

When Mrs. O'Neill requested it of me – "to relieve the atmosphere," as she put it – I played Paderewski's "Minuet"; then Wilhelm would have us listen to Massenet on a violin of choice quality. Afterward he would show me in an album scenes of his country, as well as his father's house and the home of his uncle, his father's partner. I think he was anxious to convey to me that his family was better off than you might think if you judged by him – I mean by his having had to quit his native land and come live in our small city. Yet he need have had no fear that I should form an opinion on the basis of silly social appearances; I wanted to judge people in strict accordance with their noble personal qualities. Wilhelm would explain to me how Ruisdael had really most faithfully rendered the full, sad sky of the Low Countries; and he asked me whether I thought I should like Holland enough one day to visit it. Yes, I replied; I should much like to see the canals and the tulip fields.

Then he had had sent to me from Holland a box of chocolates, each one of which was a small vial containing a liqueur.

But one evening he had the ill-starred notion of accompanying me back home, as far as our front door, though it was only two steps away and darkness had not wholly fallen. He was chivalrous: he insisted that a man should not let a woman go home all alone, even if that woman only yesterday had still been playing with hoops or walking on stilts.

Alas! The moment his back was turned, Maman asked me about my young man. "Who is that great beanstalk?"

I told her it was Wilhelm of Holland, and all the rest of it: the box of chocolates, the tulip fields, the stirring sky of Wilhelm's country, the windmills. . . . Now all that was fine and honorable! But why, despite what I thought of appearances, did I believe myself obliged also to speak of the uncle and the father, partners in a small business which . . . which . . . made a lot of money?

My mother at once forbade me to return to the O'Neills, so long, said she, as I had not got over the idea of Wilhelm.

But Wilhelm was clever. One or two days each week he finished work early; on those days he waited for me at the convent door. He took over my great bundle of books – Lord, what homework the Sisters piled on us in those days! – my music sheets, my metronome, and he carried all these burdens to the corner of our street. There he would lower upon me his large and sad blue eyes and say to me, "When you are bigger, I'll take you to the opera, to the theater. . . ."

I still had two years of the convent ahead of me; the opera, the theater seemed desperately far away. Wilhelm would tell me that he longed to see me in an evening gown: that then he would at last remove from its moth-proof bag his dress clothes and that we should go in style to hear symphonic music.

My mother ultimately learned that Wilhelm had the effrontery to carry my books, and it annoyed her very much. She forbade me to see him.

"Still," said I to Maman, "I can hardly prevent his walking next to me along the pavement."

My mother cut through that problem. "If he takes the same sidewalk as you, mind you, cross right over to the other."

Now she must have sent a message of rebuke to Wilhelm and told him, as she had me, precisely which sidewalk he should take, for I began seeing him only on the opposite side of the street, where he would stolidly await my passage. All the while I was going by, he held his hat in his hand. The other young girls must have been horribly envious of me; they laughed at Wilhelm's baring his head while I was passing. Yet I felt death in my soul at seeing Wilhelm so alone and exposed to ridicule. He was an immigrant, and Papa had told me a hundred times that you could not have too much sympathy, too much consideration for the uprooted, who have surely suffered long enough from their expatriation without adding to it, through scorn or disdain. Why then had Papa so completely changed his views, and why was he more set even than Maman against Wilhelm of Holland? True enough, no one at home, since Georgianna's marriage, looked favorably upon love. Perhaps because as a whole we had already had too much to suffer from it. But I – presumably – I had not yet suffered enough at its hands. . . .

And then, as I have said, Wilhelm was clever. Maman had forbidden him to speak to me on the street, but she had forgotten letters. Wilhelm had made great progress in English. He sent me very beautiful epistles which began with: "My own beloved child . . ." or else "Sweet little maid. . . ." Not to be outdone, I replied: "My own dearest heart. . . ." One day my mother found in my room a scrawl on which I had been practicing my handwriting and in which I expressed to

Wilhelm a passion that neither time nor cruel obstacles could bend. . . . Had my mother glanced into the volume of Tennyson lying open upon my table, she would have recognized the whole passage in question, but she was far too angry to listen to reason. I was enjoined from writing to Wilhelm, from reading his letters, if, by a miracle, one of them succeeded in penetrating the defenses thrown up by Maman; I was even enjoined from thinking of him. I was allowed only to pray for him, if I insisted upon it.

Until then I had thought that love should be open and clear, cherished by all and making peace between beings. Yet what was happening? Maman was turned into something like a spy, busy with poking about in my waste-basket; and I then thought that she was certainly the last person in the world to understand me! So that was what love accomplished! And where was that fine frankness between Maman and me! Does there always arise a bad period between a mother and her daughter? Is it love that brings it on? . . . And what, what is love? One's neighbor? Or some person rich, beguiling?

During this interval Wilhelm, unable to do anything else for me, sent me many gifts, and, at the time, I knew nothing of them, for the moment they arrived, Maman would return them to him: music scores, tulip bulbs from Amsterdam, a small collar of Bruges lace, more liqueur-filled chocolates.

The only means left to us by which to communicate was the telephone. Maman had not thought of that. Obviously she could not think of everything; love is so crafty! Then, too, during her loving days the telephone did not exist, and this, I imagine, was why Maman forgot to ban it for me. Wilhelm often called our number. If it was not I who answered, he hung up gently. And many a time did Maman then protest: "What's going on? . . . I shall write the company a letter; I'm constantly being bothered for nothing. At the other end I can barely hear a sort of sighing sound." Naturally she could not foresee how far the tenacity of a Wilhelm would extend.

But when it was I who answered, Wilhelm was scarcely better off. There could be between us no real conversation without its exposing us to the discovery of our secret and consequent prohibition of the telephone. Moreover, we neither of us had any taste for ruses; Gervais employed them when he had on the wire the darling of his heart, to whom he spoke as though she were another schoolboy. But Wilhelm and I – without blaming Gervais, for love is love, and when it encounters obstacles, is even more worthy! – we strove to be noble in all things. Thus Wilhelm merely murmured to me, from afar, "Dear heart . . ." after which he remained silent. And I listened to his silence for a minute or two, blushing to the roots of my hair.

One day, though, he discovered an admirable way to make me understand his heart. As I was saying "Allo!" his voice begged me to hold the wire; then I made out something like the sound of a violin being tuned, then the opening bars of "Thaïs." Wilhelm played me the whole composition over the phone. Kathleen must have been accompanying him. I heard piano chords somewhere in the distance, and – I know not why – this put me out a trifle, perhaps at thinking that Kathleen was in on so lovely a secret. It was the first time, however, that Wilhelm put me out at all.

Our phone was attached to the wall at the end of a dark little hallway. At first no one was surprised at seeing me spend hours there, motionless and in the most complete silence. Only little by little did the people at home begin to notice that at the telephone I uttered no word. And from then on, when I went to listen to "Thaïs," the hall door would open slightly;

someone hid there to spy on me, motioning the others to advance one by one and watch me. Gervais was the worst, and it was very mean on his part, for I had respected his secret. He manufactured reasons for making use of the hall; as he went by he tried to hear what I could be listening to. At first, however, I held the receiver firmly glued to my ear. Then I must already have begun to find "Thaïs" very long to hear through. One evening I allowed Gervais to listen for a moment to Wilhelm's music; perhaps I hoped that he would have enough enthusiasm to make me myself admire the composition. But Gervais choked with mirth; later on I saw him playing the fool in front of the others, at the far end of the living room, bowing an imaginary violin. Even Maman laughed a little, although she tried to remain angry. With a long, sad countenance which – I knew not how – he superimposed upon his own features, Gervais was giving a fairly good imitation of Wilhelm in caricature. I was a little tempted to laugh. For it is a fact that there is something quite comic in seeing a sad person play the violin.

When you consider it, it is astonishing that all of them together should not have thought much sooner of parting me from Wilhelm by the means they so successfully employed from that night forward.

All day long, when I went by, someone was whistling the melody of "Thaïs."

My brother grossly exaggerated the Dutchman's slightly solemn gait, his habit of keeping his eyes lifted aloft. They discovered in him the mien of a Protestant minister, dry – said they – and in the process of preparing a sermon. Maman added that the "Netherlander" had a face as thin as a knife blade. This was the way they now referred to him: the "Netherlander" or the "Hollander." My sister Odette – I should say Sister Edouard – who had been informed and was taking a hand in the matter, even though she had renounced the world, my pious Odette herself told me to forget the "foreigner" . . . that a foreigner is a foreigner. . . .

One evening as I listened to "Thaïs," I thought I must look silly, standing thus stock still, the receiver in my hand. I hung up before the end of the performance.

Thereafter, Wilhelm scarcely crossed my path again.

A year later, perhaps, we learned that he was returning to Holland.

My mother once more became the just and charitable pre-Wilhelm person I had loved so dearly. My father no longer harbored anything against Holland. Maman admitted that Mrs. O'Neill had told her concerning Wilhelm that he was the best man in the world, reliable, a worker, very gentle. . . . And Maman hoped that Wilhelm, in his own country, among his own people, would be loved . . . as, she said, he deserved to be.

# THE JEWELS

I must have been, perhaps, about fifteen when, quite over-
night, I went mad over jewelry. During the time I was in
the grasp of this passion, I never had enough such adorn-
ments to satisfy me; I don't think that at the time quality
counted for much in my eyes; I was too avid for anything that
sparkled, and I had not enough money to fix my yearnings on
what was handsomest. Woolworth of Winnipeg was good
enough for me. And it was in that store that one day I fell
prey to this mania, while I was trying on a necklace having the
weight and emitting the clangor of an iron chain.

I had bracelets that imitated onyx, others pretending to
be gold or diamonds; the latter were studded with hundreds
of tiny brilliants; I also had snakes coiled around my wrists,
spider brooches, horses affixed to pins, tiny dogs, cats with
closed eyes, other domestic and doubtless other repulsive
animals – certainly monkeys – and, finally, poor butterflies of
imitation mother-of-pearl with brittle glass wings. At times
I affixed almost all these pieces at once upon my chest, and I
could not decide which of them pleased me; the jewel my collection lacked always seemed to me the most desirable. Then

I would be seized with a sort of exasperation; was it really impossible, would it never be possible, at last to possess everything I needed? I was unhappy in those days.

Once from my brother Robert, who was staying with us briefly on his way through town, and who was very fond of me, I received a dollar, and rushed off to my palace of temptation. Never before had I had a whole dollar to spend all at once for adornment. The vastness of the sum, leaving the field open to my desires, made me very unsettled in my mind. At first I was tempted by a set of turtle pins; then I was drawn to some bracelets as heavy as handcuffs; then I inclined toward some false pearls. In cases of doubt, it had been my custom to settle the question by taking the most ornate; thus did I think myself proof against mistakes! But this time, if I remember well, my indecision dragged me to another shop, there to make the painful round of all available possibilities, I got little further than the cosmetics department, near the entrance door, already dazzled by the sheen of the lovely perfume bottles, of the pink or milky jars, of the slender vials in transparent pottery; but I was even more seized with admiration of the clerk at this counter, a woman of maturity, slightly faded, who displayed on her own countenance the melancholy virtues of all these products.

She must have been twice my age, perhaps even a great deal older; she had bluish eyelids, heavy black hair in which was planted a Spanish comb, remodeled eyebrows, an insensitive face, and – what was more – imprinted on that face something knowing, invulnerable, as though life could no longer harm her: something, in any case, that strongly tempted me, for I longed to resemble this woman as I have scarcely ever since wished to resemble anyone. For her it was child's play: by looking at me as though she already saw my old age looming, she made me afraid of it, and was at no pains to take my dollar in exchange for a pot of cream the size of a thimble.

Thereupon, by constantly imploring her, I persuaded Maman to buy me high-heeled shoes; I had much trouble in learning how to stand on these stilts, even more how to walk thus raised aloft. Yet I would have borne even worse tortures . . . for love of myself. Alone in my room, I would put on the shoes; I would hang from my neck a long string of many-colored glass beads, which I wrapped seven or eight times around my throat; at times it would be some other necklace, fashioned of amulets, of bits of darkened wood, of crescent and full moons; onto my arms I slipped the snake, the imitation onyx, the imitation tortoise shell, the false rubies; from my ears I hung lizards. To my waist and in my hair I affixed brilliants. Among the belongings of my eldest sister I had found face powder and lipstick. One day I fashioned myself a bloody mouth and feverish cheeks. All this accomplished, I sat down on the floor, crosslegged, in front of a Buddha, where I burned incense to myself. You placed scented strips of paper in the Buddha's body; then you lowered the head which served as lid. The smoke and the smell emerged from the replete and – as he now seems to me – sarcastic small fellow's nostrils. Whence came to me the inclination to associate him of the paunch with my uneasiness, my mad quest? He looked at me; I looked at him. I needed a witness, and it seemed to me out of the question to show myself to living persons in my transformed state. Had my father surprised me thus bedecked, he would certainly have lost his temper with a vengeance. Maman, wiser and more patient, must have hoped to see me soon cured of the disease. She would affectionately reproach me: "You were far nicer before, simple and natural, your own self! . . ." Yet perhaps she was not unaware that to be oneself is precisely the hardest of all. She gave me my head. Then, too, how should I have known who I was? This girl, unrecognizable even to my own eyes, whom I saw in my mirror, of whom I asked advice, from whom I expected a thousand surprises – this enigmatic girl, daily more outrageous – was she not momentarily the most venturesome, the truest of my various selves?

And so, crouching on the floor, in somewhat the same posture as my Buddha, I would almost choke on the vapors he belched at my face. My eyelids half closed, jewels in my hair, rings on my fingers, I watched over my poor dreams; not, surely, without a certain boredom, I would await some fresh inspiration to spring up, requiring satisfaction.

Once, knowing my father to be out, I went downstairs on my high heels, clinging for support to the banister. Then I boldly launched myself, with an excessively peculiar gait, to display my charms to my nearest and dearest. I had practiced making all my bracelets jingle at once, and I made my entrance, sparkling from head to foot, my features lofty and distant. Everyone burst out laughing. My brother Robert, who was enchanted at any foolishness on my part and who urged me on in this direction to see what I would do, stuck his hand in his pocket and produced another dollar.

"Here," he told me; "your collection must certainly lack some bit of jewelry. Take this; it'll allow you to decorate yourself even better. . . ."

But Maman sighed sorrowfully. "Why do you encourage so cruel a bent, Robert? . . ."

On my way back up to my room, I heard them talking about me. "Every woman," Maman was saying, "has, deep down within her, a poor little pagan soul, and it seems to me that you men all too often bow down before that very pagan. . . ."

"Of course," said Robert, laughing.

"She who toys with you, she who is dreaming up a thousand hard and pitiless games – yes – that's the one you egg on. When you come right down to it, there is no equality between men and women. The lovely virtues – loyalty, frankness, straightforwardness, admirable simplicity – you insist on for yourselves, whereas you esteem women for their wiles, their flightiness. And that's bad, first of all for yourselves, who are the first to suffer from it, and for women whom – it would seem – you enjoy keeping in a state of artful childishness. Oh, when, indeed," exclaimed Maman, "will the same qualities be of good repute for all! . . ."

I continued toward my room, thoughtful and forgetting to make my skirt swing, as I had learned after a fashion to do. Once more I saw my smoking Buddha, an ugly, fat little man, basically repugnant. Once again I sat down as before, my legs folded under me, my eyes searching myself out in the mirror . . . but my pagan soul had nothing left to offer me. Come! Was that all she expected of me: to steal a bit of powder, to paint my mouth, to cover myself with a nasty collection of jingling trinkets, only to leave me yawning, lazy, and disappointed? And how could I have been this barbarian, this child, this slave?

Abruptly I tore from my arms the onyx, the coiled snake, the brilliants, of which a good half had already fallen from their cheap settings. I threw them into the bottom of the scrap basket; there also followed the Buddha, an accomplice perhaps, but perhaps likewise an indulgent Censor. I poured into the washbasin the rest of my perfumes. Suddenly – I wanted equality on earth, and I rubbed my cheeks so hard with soap that they burned.

Naturally I could not yet do better than go from one extreme to the other: I smoothed my hair and smoothed it yet again, in order to do away forever with any natural curliness. And then I cast myself upon my knees; I did penance. But my soul was still distempered: did it not insist, and that at once, that I should leave for Africa to nurse the lepers?

# THE VOICE OF THE POOLS

I n the pools not far from our house, some evening toward
April, began a kind of piercing, vibrant music, softly sad
withal, which lasted almost all summer, only to cease
whenever the water in these pools had been wholly consumed
by the sun or by the earth.

The tiny singers – hundreds of frogs – were invisible.
Emerging from winter, from their numbness, from the mud,
did they recapture this thin, strident voice to talk to each
other, to greet each other from one swamp to another? Or
else did they live once more, did they free themselves from the
viscous bottom only to stir our hearts a while with a strange
music? At first individual, scattered, in the end these voices
harmonized and soon made up a single long and continuous
cry. I still hear it, drilling through the spring nights around our
home; never have I heard a stronger summons toward childhood, toward its somewhat savage joys.

I still often went to my attic, even when I became a hard-
working student, even when I was a little older and on the

edge of what is called youth. What did I go up there for? I was perhaps sixteen on the evening when I climbed there as though in search of myself. What should I be, later on? . . . What should I do with my life? . . . Yes, such were the questions I was beginning to ask myself. Probably I thought the time had come to reach decisions regarding my future, regarding that person all unknown to me who would one day be I.

And it happened that that evening, as I leaned out of the little attic window toward the cry of the pools close by, there appeared to me – if one may say that they appear – those vast, somber lands which time spreads before us. Yes, such was the land that lay stretched in front of me – vast, wholly mine, yet wholly to be discovered.

The frogs, that evening, had swollen their voices to the point of making them a cry of distress, a cry of triumph as well . . . as though they foretold a parting. I then saw, not what I should later become, but that I must set forth on my way to becoming it. It seemed to me that I was at once in the attic and also far away – in the loneliness of the future; and that from yonder, committed at so great a distance, I was showing myself the road, I was calling myself and saying to myself, "Yes, come, this is the way I must travel. . . ."

And so I had the idea of writing. What and why I knew not at all. I would write. It was like a sudden love which, in a moment, binds a heart; it was really a fact as simple, as naïve as love. Having as yet nothing to say . . . I wanted to have something to say.

Did I try my hand at it instantly? Did I at once obey this outlandish command? A gentle wind of spring was blowing my hair, the thousand frog voices filled the night, and I wanted to write as one feels the need to love, to be loved. It was still vague, beneficent, a bit sad, too. All round me were the books of my childhood, which here I had read and reread, in a dancing beam of dusty light, pouring down like a ray of sun from the gable window. And the happiness the books had given me I wished to repay. I had been the child who reads hidden from everyone, and now I wanted myself to be this beloved book, these living pages held in the hands of some nameless being, woman, child, companion, whom I would keep for myself a few hours. Is there any possession equal to this one? Is there a friendlier silence, a more perfect understanding?

Yet, this other myself, who in the future urged me to attain her, that other myself – oh, the bliss of ignorance! – was clothed as I was that evening in a navy-blue serge blouse, with a broad sailor collar; she had the same slightly thoughtful young face, leaning in the hollow of one hand; she had grown no older.

My mother one evening came to find me in this low-ceilinged chamber, where I so constantly remained, fascinated by the thousand sounds of the night which I was learning to distinguish one from another, fascinated – beyond daring aught else – by the breadth, the mystery of the task I had assigned myself, or else had accepted to undertake. The song of the pools was growing weaker; now, separate one from the other; the little voices sought each other, seemed to reply to one another, or – perchance – to draw apart. . . .

Maman asked me, "Why do you forever shut yourself up here? It doesn't go with your years. You should be playing tennis or having fun with your friends. You've gotten quite pale. And yet these are the best days of your life. Why not put them to better use?"

Thereupon I solemnly announced to Maman what was

transpiring; that I was to write. . . . For this, was it not neces-sary to come to the attic, listen for a long, long while to the intermingling voices . . . and so many things you must untangle?

Maman seemed upset. It was, nevertheless, her fault if I preferred fiction to daily life. She had taught me the power of images, the wonder of a thing revealed by just the right word, and all the love that one simple and beautiful sentence may contain.

"Writing" she told me sadly, "is hard. It must be the most exacting business in the world . . . if it is to be true, you understand! Is it not like cutting yourself in two, as it were – one half trying to live, the other watching, weighing? . . ."

And she went on: "First the gift is needed; if you have not that, it's heartbreak; but if you have it, it's perhaps equally terrible. . . . For we say the gift; but perhaps it would be better to say the command. And here is a very strange gift," Maman continued, "not wholly human. I think other people never forgive it. This gift is a little like a stroke of ill luck which with-draws others, which cuts us off from almost everyone. . . ."

How could Maman speak with such exact knowledge? As she talked I felt the truth of what she said, and felt as though I had already suffered it.

Maman's eyes were distant, and she was so concerned to guard me well, to defend me, that they filled with sadness. "To write," she said to me, "is this not, finally, to be far from others . . . to be all alone, poor child?"

After a brief rain, the frogs renewed their song of such fetching wearisomeness. I think one must yearn far in advance for the long road to be traveled, for the ultimate visage which will give us life. Curiosity to know ourselves – perhaps that is what best draws us forward. . . .

"At times words also succeed in being true," said I to Maman. "And without words, would there be a single truth of which you could say: Thus it is; it's true!"

Then Maman made a gesture so desolate, so powerless. She said as she went away, "The future is a terrible thing. It is always something of a defeat."

She left me to the night, to the lonely attic, to the vast sorrow of the land of blackness.

But I still hoped that I could have everything: both a warm and true life, like a shelter – at times, too, unbearable with harsh truth – and also time to capture its reverberation in the depths of the soul; time to walk, and time to halt that I might understand; time to withhold myself a little along the road, and then to catch up with the others, to rejoin them and to cry joyously, "Here I am, and here is what I've found for you along the way! Have you waited for me? . . . Aren't you waiting for me? Oh, do wait for me! . . ."

# THE STORM

Winters in Manitoba, at my uncle's dear, beautiful farm, when we were sixteen . . . did we sleep on holiday eves, when the sun as it set had taken on a worrisome color? Often we would wake up and listen – with distrustful ear – lest the wind growl too hard over the roof, and then we would sleep briefly, pulling the good woolen blankets up to our chins.

Now, this holiday morning, we had seen when we got up that the snow fallen the day before lay quiet; it clung to the soil, asleep as it lay, like a big motionless cat making a muff of its paws. Rays of sunshine everywhere caught the weary animal's blinking eyes. And we thought – my cousin Rita, her two brothers, Philippe and Adrien, and I, who was spending my vacation with them – that nothing could prevent us from going to the gathering of all the neighborhood youth that was to take place at the home of my cousin's friends the Guérins, whom I did not know, but who surely would be lovely people! . . . How ready was I to like these people I had never met, with whom we were to join forces after dashing over a dozen miles of appalling road!

We had decided to leave toward four in the afternoon, allowing ourselves two hours for the trip, since we were supposed to be there for supper. As for our return, were we worried? It would certainly take place during the small hours of the following night, amidst glacial cold. No matter! What mattered was to get going, and we clasped hands, my cousins and I, and danced through the house, singing our heads off. My poor aunt, then quite ill, had begged us to restrain a little our happiness – at least not to make quite so much noise over it.

Toward two, the sky grew almost completely dark. From my uncle Nicolas's house, built in the heart of a little woods, we could now only make out the nearest poplar trees, standing very close to the porch: small trees reaching bleak branches toward a day which, little by little, like a fog, swallowed the trees' gestures, then the trees themselves. Soon we might have thought ourselves no longer dwelling in a house surrounded by woods, but situated wherever you might fancy it, in some unknown land; a mountain house, perhaps, so cut off had it become! And the snow began to stretch itself along the ground, then to fly, to surge up, to fill all the air. My cousin Philippe, however, laughingly said that he so perfectly knew the road to the Guérins' that it would take more than this powdering gale to prevent him from driving us there.

The next question was what vehicle we should use. At my uncle's there were several means of winter travel: first, the old Ford, its canvas curtains adorned with small squares of mica; but it was little used, since in those days snowplows did not exist to open the roads; then there were the long sleds with several seats; the cutter, a much smaller sleigh, very low on its runners, that skimmed along like a cloud, but could not hold us all comfortably; and finally there was the "cabin."

This it was we determined to take, since the cold was increasing.

Oh, the good "cabin" of those bygone days!

It was a sort of little house, somewhat higher than it was wide, with a door at the back, a slot in front through which passed the reins, and above this a glass panel. Inside were two benches, either facing each other or built transversely across the "cabin's" breadth. Occasionally a small stove was installed within, its pipe passing through an opening in the ceiling to carry away the smoke. And surely nothing could be prettier in those days than to see advancing across the frozen countryside these tiny, smoking houses, which you knew to be filled with muffled people coming from afar to land on one's very own doorstep! My uncle's, though, had had no stove ever since a bump on the road had one day dumped everything, including the live coals, upon the floor, and the fire had driven the passengers outside to risk death from the cold.

How comfortable it was, though, our "cabin," built of sturdy balsam planks, lined inside with a heavy brown wrapping paper, and complete with its two upholstered seats! It had, indeed, its inconveniences, of which the principal one – from our point of view – was not enough speed; for, driven too fast, its top-heaviness could cause it to overturn; besides, it churned us up so thoroughly that we would emerge covered with bruises. But the fun of being in there, all huddled together!

Toward half past three, thinking to get ahead of the real blow, we laughingly stowed ourselves away under our warm buffalo robes, heated bricks at our feet.

My uncle was out of sorts. Forgetful of the time when he himself had made a beeline for every dance within twenty miles, he grumbled that we would do better to stick close to the fire on a day like this; that, in any case, if go we must, at least we should take a sleigh rather than this "cabin" from which we could make out neither the turns in the road nor any landmark along our way.

But Philippe tightened the reins and the "cabin" lurched off. Now were we hurled against one another, laughing, disentangling ourselves, banging our noses against each other. Though we were traveling across flat country, this vehicle staggered so thoroughly over every slightest bump, every lump of snow, that it created for us the illusion – charming on our level plains – of being dragged up and down the steepest of mountain roads.

While we were still on the lane leading to the farm, my cousin Philippe could vaguely make out the edge of the woodland, but once upon the public highway, there was no longer anything to guide us, for the trees were far from the road and we could see nothing of them. Moreover, the little glass panel had entirely frosted over. And, indeed, what could we have seen, even had we been in the open?

A very weak glow, vaguely the color of *café au lait*, for a short while longer filtered through the glass panel; then this minimal sign of daylight faded away. It was barely four o'clock and we were smothered in darkness.

We now lighted a lantern, which we tried to hang from its hook in the ceiling. But our gyrations constantly threatening to tumble it upon our heads, in the end we, turn and turn about, held it in our hands. Having very shortly observed that its glow – according to the angle at which it was held – distorted, transformed our faces, we made merry by swinging the lantern, by moving it from one place to another, to laugh the more heartily at the unexpected results we thus obtained.

Meanwhile, it was getting colder; we all put on our

mittens and drew tighter around our necks our heavy woolen scarves.

Philippe, glued to the panel, gave up trying to see anything outside. He gave the horses free rein, saying that they themselves would certainly make their own way to the crucial intersection; there, at the crossroads, we should find the telephone line; and we would only have to follow it, from pole to pole, until we reached the Guérins'. . . . Child's play!

And the four of us began to tell each other something of what we were going to do later on, when we should be on our own and wholly free. Philippe announced that he would have a very large restaurant with a jazz band – a farfetched idea which, of course, he never followed up. For his part, Adrien, already a trifle peevish and bitter – but also less handsome than Philippe – seemed more to wish for the happiness of others than to elaborate one to his own measure; and he let it be understood that if he had this, or else that, he'd know how to turn it to his advantage. Rita, the shrewd dreamer, said she would never marry . . . because boys were too stupid. And I, nestling against my cousin Rita, of whom I was so fond, indeed wholly beguiled by my three young cousins – the warmth of our friendship as vivid to me as that of their bodies – I proposed to them: "Why don't we choose, rather, to die together before we get old, ugly, and crabbed. Nothing could be simpler! All we have to do is set out on foot through this gale. . . ."

My cousin shivered a little and she protested that we surely had time to live a bit longer before becoming ugly and ill-tempered . . . that at least we'd first go to the party, wouldn't we?

At this juncture the "cabin" jolted heavily, as though we were attempting a sudden slope, and then came to a halt.

We had stopped laughing. Was it because of my proposal, because it suddenly occurred to us that my aunt was very ill? Each of us looked anxiously at the other, as though seeking a denial of the ideas that flashed through our minds. But we all betrayed the same tense faces and bated breaths.

Philippe opened the door, and the wind pounced on us inside the "cabin" like a demon unleashed.

Outside, Philippe cried, "Come and see . . . what you make of it! . . ."

One by one we got out, leaning against the wind, suffocated and almost blinded by its violence. Like fiery needles the snow pricked our eyes. Yet had we, despite everything, been able to hold them open, what could we have seen? Nothing belongs more fully to the wind than snow – so docile, so malleable! And here was the wind holding suspended in the air all that swollen snowy dust. Oh, the fine play of black and white commingled!

The exhilaration storms always roused in me was too strong to allow the feeling of danger to outweigh it. As I stood near the "cabin," I listened to the wind, first of all intent to grasp what it was saying, to define its great, crashing cymbals, then its poor, plaintive wail, so long drawn out. With no other instrument than itself, how could the wind produce such a variety of sounds, an orchestra complete, at times, with outbursts of laughter and of pain? Much later, when it was granted me to hear the Walkyries' cries, I told myself that here truly is the music of the wind heard in other days, when its myriad snow steeds dashed in full career over Manitoba.

Philippe, a little older than we, became anxious.

"Where can we be? . . . Anyway, let's stick together; if we even lose sight of each other for a second . . . well . . ."

Then he said to his brother, "Come help me clear a little snow. We must have left the road. I think we are in a furrow. If we find one under the snow, at least we'll know that much. . . ."

Two paces away from him I could barely hear the sound of his voice.

Whereupon the wind started to weep in so sorrowful, so absurd a fashion that of a sudden I thought of the beautiful Archangel cast into darkness – for thus had he been called aforetime. And I firmly believed that the wind was Lucifer, to whom, for a winter's night or two, belonged Manitoba!

My two cousins, shaking with the cold, were trying to fathom the configuration of the soil; they said that they thought they could distinguish massive ridges beneath the snow, which might indicate a plowed field. But what did that tell us? Were there not plowed fields on any farm?

"Everybody," said Adrien in a tone of pessimism, "plows in the fall. . . ."

His voice trailed off as he drew away a few steps. Suddenly I was grasped by the arms; I was pulled toward a human shape as vague as my own; lips pressed on mine, damp with snow. From the young mustache I knew it was Philippe whose heart beat next to me. For a long while in the wind which labored furiously to tear us apart did he thus hold me to himself. But when the others drew near, he let me go. When he spoke, his voice seemed to have aged, become in a few moments as serious as that of a man. "Let's keep on going; perhaps the horses on their own will take us back to the road."

Again piled into the "cabin," now cold as a tomb, moving where the horses saw fit, for almost an hour we journeyed, but now in silence. And then, once more, the strange jolting, the two or three heavy bumps, the full stop!

We were very cold. It made our shoulders shudder. We emerged anew from the "cabin" in brief single file, each holding hard to the coattails of another. And we strove to recognize, in the lee of the gale, some aspect of reality. I kept my eyes open despite the snow; it was like a flame, piercing your eyeballs. Meanwhile, everything that was not exposed to its burning – one's feet, one's back, one's hands – froze. Whereupon I made out something of a vague and melancholy shape, resembling a fearful, lost home, never inhabited, never with light at its windows, a dreadful ghost of a dwelling.

We walked toward this terrible black house and, after a dozen steps, we touched it with our outstretched hands. What could it be? Under our fingers it was moist, lacking solidity and resistance. . . . Then a great burst of laughter set us free: the thing we had approached and surrounded with such fear was no more than a great pile of straw.

But such straw ricks were likewise everywhere, on all farms. What could be learned from the shape of this one?

"It might belong to the Labossières . . . the Frenettes . . . the Frenchman . . . the Scotchman. . . to anyone . . ." Philippe counted them off. "Let's get going again. What's important is not to let ourselves be frozen."

Before re-entering the "cabin," I journeyed as far as our horses' heads, guiding myself along their streaming flanks. Oh, their poor eyes! The vapors emitted by their nostrils and the natural liquid around their eyeballs had frozen fast their eyelids; weighted with ice, they could no longer open. Breathing upon their heads, warming our hands with our breaths and then applying them to this ice, we little by little set free their living eyes, which betrayed only the mildest surprise and fluttered a little as they focused upon us. . . . Then forward once more!

Our horses walked for a long while, as though more sure of themselves, leaning their heads one against the other, probably to lend each other courage. We were drowsy, and Philippe was constantly shaking us. "You mustn't fall asleep," said he; "fight the cold. . . ." And here was the hardest part of that night!

Later when, once more come to a halt, we had again seen that strange and sinister black structure standing in the snow, we did not fear it. But was this the same stack of straw we had already driven by or another?

"It must be the same one," said Philippe. "When they cannot see, horses go in a circle."

Then a kind of despair overcame Adrien.

"We're going to keep everlastingly coming back to this pile of straw," he complained. "It's inevitable."

And he told of a farmer who, last winter – or was it two years earlier? – had lost his way on such a night while merely crossing from his home to his farm buildings.

"Shut up," Philippe ordered him.

But the idiot kept citing tragic instances, one after the other.

"Let's stay here. . . ."

"Where can we be? . . ."

"How many miles away? . . ."

Our thoughts were reduced to mere questions.

And suddenly I cried out in anguish, "Rita! Rita! Rita!" because, for perhaps half a minute, I had not heard her voice mingled with the others'. Whereupon from far away a voice answered me, "I'm here . . ." and at the same moment my cousin's hand touched my own. Out of our joy we embraced with all the awkwardness of blind people.

A little later, over a wave of snow, I believed I saw a slight glimmer; then at once it disappeared and I mistrusted my eyes. None the less I told the others, "Over there – far away – I think I saw a light! . . ."

The four of us, studious together, long stared into this whirlpool of snow.

And again, like the riding lights of a ship one glimpses when a high wave lifts it out of the abyss, I espied the pale glow. Adrien also had perceived it, having through some amazing circumstance fastened his gaze at the same moment as I upon the same infinitely small point in this horizonless infinity.

He cried out, "Yes, yes, yes! It's true! There is a light over there!"

Leading our horses by their bridles, we walked toward this light, which we never again saw all together, but singly and by turns. After five minutes, the light seemed to me a bit more certain, easier to spot. Almost at the same time I crashed into a tree.

"Trees! . . . Hereabouts!" exclaimed Philippe, quickly shifting from astonishment to reflection and then reassurance.

There immediately loomed up a towering house shape, still very indefinite and far away.

"The building looks square," said Rita joyfully.

"All the houses around here are square," growled Adrien. Then he stopped growling and quickened his pace, whistling under his breath.

A few more steps and we had circumnavigated the dark side of the square house. Our horses tried to get away from us. A lighted window showed its square through the night. And at last we saw the lamp in its place on a shelf, then – not far off – the face of the old clock reflecting the light; the rocking chair, too, and probably the cat asleep on her cushion – every-thing as it should be!

Holding a lamp at the level of his eyes, my uncle appeared on the doorsill. His face betrayed his content at seeing us back home and surprise at finding us so little upset.

"Come in, come in, you gang of young fools! I was quite sure in my mind you'd turn back . . . At last you've come to your senses, you silly little idiots! . . ."

# BY DAY AND BY NIGHT

My father, so sad and withdrawn during the day, toward night began somewhat to revive. You might have thought that the sun as it set, the daylight as it faded, freed him of a dreadful verity which he ceaselessly carried before his eyes. Was it that he constantly kept seeing the day when, on his return from a trip to his settlements, he stopped in at his office in Winnipeg to pick up the mail and found this letter addressed to him: "For which reason we ask you kindly to offer your resignation . . . realize the value of your services, the devotion of your life to the settlers, of whom several have spoken in your behalf. . . . But other circumstances . . . The new law regarding the retirement age . . ."? From its first reading, I think my father must have known this letter by heart, and perhaps he never succeeded in driving the words from his mind. He went through a few ridiculous days during which, urged on by my mother and by friends, he tried to appeal his case to the government, but he had not enough confidence in himself to undertake the visits, the pleas to which he would have had to agree. And maybe he was especially repelled by the idea – monstrous to him – of having to display his merits, his life. For with this letter, not only had he no longer confidence in what he was, in what he could do, but he even lost the feeling of ever having been useful. By this letter he was in a sense stripped of all his achievements, and he kept on living only to bear the daily weight of this defeat upon his shoulders. Happily the night was still gentle to him. When it came, so simple and sweet-smelling along our street, my father greeted it like a familiar guest. Was this a merely physical well-being? Or had this hour still sufficient empire over his soul to revive within it hope of happiness? Whatever the case, this phenomenon was so familiar to each of us that, if we wished to obtain my father's permission for something we wanted, we waited – as Maman advised – "until it is dark."

But Maman was a creature of the day. I have never seen anyone so impatient to get up in the morning to go out in summer at the sun's first rays in order to care for her flowers, which were as full of health as Maman herself. She took it very ill that we should sleep late, and if her kindliness forbade her to make noise for fear of waking us, soon her vitality overcame her caution – or perchance it was her unconscious desire to make us get up which led to her clattering the saucepans. Even in winter she arose very early to light the fires, now that my father was so ailing, and to set the porridge to boil; then, in bitter cold, and through darkness, Maman trotted off to the earliest Mass. When we got up, the house was already warm, a going concern, its sleepiness well shaken off. Yes, Maman's activities were full to overflowing as long as they were accompanied and sustained by daylight; but the moment dusk fell, she abruptly lost all her momentum; she would yawn; never did she show her age except in the evening, under the harsh electric light. She put me in mind of those flowers, so living by day which at night so sadly hang their heads. And toward ten o'clock, if we expected no company, if there were nothing extraordinary to revive Maman in her overpowering drowsiness, she would say to us, "Well, I'm going to bed; I'm dropping on my feet." And she would beg us, "Do try not to stay up until some impossible hour."

It was one of her ideas that to be in good health you must retire early, rise early; that sitting up by electric light ruined one's eyes.

At this hour, however, Papa was just coming back to life. Yes, he greatly helped himself with coffee which he made very strong, and indeed very good, as compared to Maman's dishwater. Thus it happened that evening, while he was watching his coffee on the stove and its aroma was spreading everywhere, that Papa glanced at Maman.

"Already!"

He was always as astonished at seeing Maman go to bed come ten o'clock as she was to see him sleep almost all day.

Maman arose to leave us. And although she had lived with father for thirty-six years and must have known that her recommendations and reproaches were unavailing with him, on that evening as on every other Maman said to my father, "Really, Edouard, I don't understand you, drinking coffee at ten o'clock! What's more, it isn't even coffee, but essence of coffee! It's no wonder that afterward you are fidgety, that you should be ill and unable to sleep! You turn night into day!"

My father made no answer to this ancient reproach. In the daytime he might have made a fairly biting rejoinder. But at this hour he grew indulgent, even though he more and more obstinately followed his own sweet will: the ease night brought him was too precious to him for him to be able to give it up. Most likely he was ready, were it necessary, to pay for it with what remained to him of health, of life. At times, watching my father, I would already say to myself, "It's not so much to life that he clings, that many others cling, maybe, as it is to certain rare and brief moments in life. . . ."

"Well, then, go!" said he to Maman. "Seeing you can sleep with the hens. I don't know how you do it. . . . Go sleep, poor Maman!"

For, now that he was very old, she much younger than he, like all of us he called her "Maman."

This evening, however, my mother seemed more resolved than ever to prevent my father's having his way. A terrible weariness spread over her face, as though she could truly no longer endure seeing him so little careful of his health, hastening – you might say – his end. She must have done herself a real violence not to register a final reproach, a last prayer; she began to move away, her arms hanging by her sides. Still young, I realized how desperate a business it is to be in the right concerning those one loves.

With her hand Maman made me a brief sign which meant, "Don't you be too late. You, at least, could follow my example. . . ." And was she, by this poor little gesture, asking me to remain her ally?

I was myself hesitating as between day and night. Like Maman, I felt, when I had gone to bed early, a joyous haste to greet the dawn, to run to my open window; I inherited from her that feeling of possession for things which in so many human beings is a product of the morning: the world seemed then to me as though at its beginning. Here was a new slate on which to write my life. I got up with my head full of resolutions: to give my hair a hundred brush strokes, to put a fresh collar on my convent uniform, to go over my homework. . . . Then, again, if I stayed up a little late, if I succeeded in repelling the first assaults of sleep, I would attain a kind of overexcitement very different from the fine calm of morning – but how wonderful! Morning seemed to me the time of logic, night of something perhaps truer than logic. . . . In any case, I was far older than my years as far as the evening went, and possessed an understanding beyond my experience. I had noticed that the words and sentences of my compositions flowed quite easily in the morning; but thought itself – or rather that nimbus which surrounds it while it is still unshaped and precious – I experienced at night. I was divided between these two sides of my nature, which came to me from my parents, sundered by the day and the night.

I lingered on for some time that evening with Papa. To induce us to stay with him, he would practice such obvious wiles. First he would offer us some of his black coffee, as well as toast which he made with a long fork over the coals. And if, through these halting advances, we were kept from hurrying elsewhere, then – sometimes – it happened that my father began to talk – and the full effect of the coffee aroused in him a sort of sparkling lucidity, precise, vivid, and very well-chosen words. The few times when he told me of his life were on such occasions, almost in the dark, alongside the stove now barely warm.

Once he had led me into the small room that contained his old roll-top desk and his wall maps of the colonization regions. As they were very detailed and large scale, a single corner of Saskatchewan covered a wall. That particular evening he unrolled one of them and showed me where he had formerly established some tenscore Mennonites. He spoke of "my people, my settlers," and likewise, "my immigrants," stressing the possessive pronoun so that this word "immigrant," rather than signifying a stranger, took on a curious value of blood relationship. "Here," he would say, "I found them a heavy layer of black earth, true gumbo, the soil that best suits wheat, and it yielded them sixty bushels to the acre." He pulled the string on another map, and with his finger pointed out the location of a Galician hamlet founded by him. I date my passion for maps from the time when my father made me behold upon them the low-lying little houses of the plain, some new dwelling place in emptiness . . . perhaps even the people themselves, inside their homes, gathered around the table. At least once my father grew spirited enough to relive, in front of the map, his long voyages of other days – and perhaps it made him forget, for a few moments, *the* letter: "Have to replace you with a younger man . . . necessary to apply the most up-to-date methods . . ." – that letter which set forth so many reasons in order not to have to give the only real one, and the one which would have been the least wounding: "We must hand over your job to a man of the right political party. . . . What we need is not a servant of the country, but a servant of our own. . . ."

In this little study of my father's there was also a full-length portrait of Sir Wilfrid Laurier. It showed the statesman in an attitude that must have been habitual with him while he was speaking in public: the high forehead lifted, as though illumined by a thought that had just come into being, the right hand open to present the evidence, the long hair, white and supple, floating behind as though in a breeze. And Papa said to me of Laurier: "Whatever words may be spoken about him, remember that this man labored to unite Canadians, never to divide them – and that's the best tribute you can pay a man when he's conquered and beaten, when he's dead."

Oh, had I been better able to sit up at night, I should better have learned to know my father! But I was unaware then that a somewhat more patient attention on my part would have freed him from silence.

The last time he talked to us, it was; I believe, about Verigin. "The Dukhobors," explained my father, "thought that Verigin, their leader, was Christ reincarnate, that they could never be wrong if they heeded his words. Poor people! To such an extent bewitched by Verigin they did not see his faults; or rather, seeing him, they believed only in him; to their Little Father Verigin, all was permitted, since he was of divine essence. . . . For one does not impute evil to God! So Verigin could exact from them the harshest penances, abstinence, continence, whereas he himself! . . . I saw him occasionally: he was richly clad, well-fed, surrounded by young girls. He traveled only with an escort of young maidens dressed in white, bedecked with flowers. Oh, we were long fooled by him! He played a double game, claiming to make his people subject to the country's laws, to work with Ottawa, whereas more and more he pushed his adepts toward a crazy mysticism. I should have liked to have known him better, grasp the devil's part, maybe, in this strange nature, understand the dark satisfaction he can have felt in obtaining from others more than from himself."

Thereupon Agnès complained, "Lord, Papa! How late it is! And tomorrow I must help Maman with the house cleaning."

And yet she liked, more than anyone else, to hear Papa tell about the country, the past, and she loved to see him forget his sorrows. But with such delicate health, sitting up late wore her out, and she insisted on husbanding her strength to help Maman as much as possible. Little by little, through her own efforts and almost joyously, she had fashioned for herself at home a very useful little niche, by no means brilliant, even dull. Martha's part, if you will. That evening she must have undergone a long struggle against fatigue and the headaches so constantly hers.

"Papa, half past eleven!"

My father drew his big watch from his pocket. "Not at all, Agnès; only eleven!"

"You know very well, Papa, that we set our clock by the church, when the Angelus rang."

"Sometimes they are ahead of time, even at the church."

But it was obvious that his spirits had been quenched by all these remarks about the hour. He looked at Agnès anxiously "True enough," said he, "you are pale and your face is drawn. You're failing . . . you, too, Agnès."

She went to him and kissed his forehead, then moved away, leaning against the furniture out of sheer weariness.

We remained alone, Papa and I, in the feeble glow of the stove. Even on summer nights he kept it, as he said, "just alive," for often enough was not the fire his sole companion? He offered me some of his coffee.

"Just for once!" said he. "A little cup; I don't think it will do you any harm."

And he deceived himself so skillfully, he so ably bent truth to his own purposes, that he announced, with deep seriousness, "I never found that coffee prevented me from sleeping; it merely helps you to remember better, to sort your impressions, and sometimes also to recapture flavors, names, maybe a soul that is not so old. . . ."

I accepted a cup, which he brought me steaming to the table corner where I had rested my elbows. Despite myself, my eyes were closing. With some slight remorse I thought of my unfinished homework, of the approaching examinations. I drank a little coffee.

"I diluted it a bit for you," said my father, "which is bad, for coffee does not stand baptising. Your mother really should try it; then she could sit up a little later nights. . . ."

"But Maman is out of bed at five in the morning, Papa!"

"Yes," said he. "That's something I've never understood, that at the very crack of dawn your mother should feel such a need of bustling about."

I had never heard Papa talk in this almost teasing, joking way. In the dark cosiness of the kitchen, with all the doors shut, he walked back and forth, his hands behind him, limber, full of plans. When he turned toward me, once, a sudden spurt of flame in the fire showed me the brilliance of his eyes; I saw them overflowing with confidence. But also I saw his bent back, the dreadful lines which life had etched into his face. And it was surely at that moment that I thought, "Why, Papa is a broken man!"

Abruptly he asked me, "Little one, what do you think of an idea I have? Your mother has no faith in my ideas. But: after all, even at seventy-two, one can still be useful . . . within limits. . . ."

He sat down close to me, as though to establish that I had become an adult in his eyes; I felt as though I had a child beside me, a sad, unruly child.

"I still have a little – a very little – money," my father confided to me, "a little remainder of what I once earned. Were I to buy a business, a grocery store, don't you think it would bring in something? We should take turns at the counter; I myself would be there the most frequent of all. I think," said he, "I have a talent for dealing with people. . . ."

It was so farfetched: Papa a shopkeeper, he who now fled people's company, he whom we had to nurse all day, who could scarcely stir after his nocturnal vigils! Only toward six in the morning, his exaltation spent, did he sleep, at times as though in an abyss, his terrible defeat written in the folds of his half-open mouth, in his ravaged features.

He continued telling me about his schemes. "If I have only six months to live, it would be better to stretch our savings as far as we can; but if I have still several years left, would it not be wise to invest the little money remaining to us? Perhaps – for instance – in a mushroom farm? . . ."

I could barely follow what he was saying. I was so tired that instead of stimulating me the coffee had made me drowsier.

"Papa, it's past midnight!"

"Midnight," he exclaimed, and added – he who found the years interminable – "Heavens! How time flies! . . ."

"Tomorrow I have a class I haven't yet prepared for . . . in contemporary history."

"Oh yes! Contemporary history," he repeated somberly. "Of course. You're still going to school!"

He seemed fearfully unhappy to have to cede so simple a fact, maybe to be reminded of his own age.

"One shouldn't have children when one is old," he said to me, his head bowed. "One can quit this world without knowing them, without knowing much about them, and that's a heartbreaking loss. . . ."

Suddenly he asked me, "Could you not stay with me another hour?"

At the moment, I grasped but the bare meaning of his rather unreasonable request. Only later did the precise words recur to me. . . . And the exams soon to be taken, the scholastic success to be won, the good grades, my future, if you like – I had one to prepare for, as people say – yes, it must have been my future which intervened at that moment between my father and me. I told him, "Papa, it would be more sensible for you to go to bed rather than sit up all night. You can't do anything useful during the day if you've not slept well."

"You talk just like your mother," was his reply.

But he took pity on me: "Poor child! You're asleep on your feet! . . . Oh well, go; get your rest." Yet in the same breath he accused me with a sort of bitterness: "You're all like her, down deep. Even you. She has you all to herself . . . that Maman of yours! . . ."

Moved by loyalty to Maman, I replied, "Surely you wouldn't have us behave the way you do!"

"Oh no!" he at once agreed. "Certainly not!"

And I saw him accept, his eyes wide open, his madness of solitude.

He poured himself another cup of black coffee. Like Maman, I thought, "There's nothing for it; he's resolved to be his own undoing." I went up to bed. Perhaps he wandered about the whole night long. For thus it was when we left him; he would pace the downstairs hall, then to and fro in the kitchen. His peregrinations would even make him forget to mend the fire. Sometimes, waking in the night, I would hear that regular, monotonous tread, the tread of a man too actively engaged in his mind, perhaps launched upon one of those illusions which make men take themselves off into the desert.

The next day he was unable to quit his bed. He was completely worn out. He would not speak much of the great pain he was beginning to suffer; perhaps he had already been having these attacks a long time. Uncomplaining, but with his usual stubbornness, he would say, "It's true. I can't stand it any longer. Give me something to lessen the pain a bit. I'm too old to be able to put up with it any longer. . . ." They had to give him morphine.

His liver was completely used up. Once or twice more he asked for coffee, at about the hour when it had been his habit to drink some, and the doctor said to Maman, "What difference can it make now?"

But in the end coffee also betrayed his faith and brought him only nausea.

At night Maman sat up with him. But she was so contrary to the hours of darkness that, despite her worry, despite her distress over my father's inert form, she would bend her head a little and, like a child, slip briefly into the haven of sleep . . . until pain once more claimed her.

My father died at the hour that was the most cruel for him, when the sun rises over the earth.

## TO EARN MY LIVING . . .

One evening in my tiny attic room, which I had whitewashed and which was austere in color, but crazy, too – stuffed with incongruous baggage – and just the way I wanted it, in this my refuge, Maman appeared, out of breath from her rapid ascent of two flights of stairs. She glanced about, seeking a place to sit, for I insisted that chairs were dull and would have only cushions scattered over the floor. I played the artist, still unaware that a writer is the most self-sufficient of beings – or the most lonely! – and that he could just as readily write in a desert, if in a desert he should still feel the need to communicate with his fellows. Be this as it may, I sought to create an "atmosphere" for myself, and Maman was abashed every time she penetrated into what she called my "mumbo jumbo." Yet was this surprising? In those days I was forever abashed at myself. Maman, very uncomfortable upon a narrow bench, at once broached the subject that had brought her. "Christine," she asked me, "have you considered what you're going to do with your life? Here you are in your last year of school. Have you given it any thought?"

"But I've told you, Maman. I should like to write . . . ."

"I'm talking seriously, Christine. You're going to have to choose an occupation." Her lips trembled slightly. "Earn your living . . ."

Of course I had already often heard this phrase, but it had never seemed that it might some day fully apply to me. It was upon this evening that its words dedicated me to solitude. To earn one's living! How mean, it seemed to me, how selfish, how grasping! Must life be earned? Was it not better to make a gift of it once for all, in some beautiful impulse? Or even to lose it? Or – again – to stake it, to gamble it . . . Oh, anything! But to earn it, pettily, day by day! . . . That evening it was exactly as though someone had told me, "For the mere fact that you live, you must pay."

I think I never made a more disconsolate discovery: all life subject to money, every dream appraised in terms of its yield.

"Oh, maybe I'll earn my living by writing . . . a little later . . . before too long. . . ."

"You poor girl!" said my mother; and after a silence, after a sigh, she continued, "Wait first until you have lived! You've plenty of time. But in the meantime, in order to live, what do you expect to do? . . ."

Then she confessed to me, "Almost all the former earnings left by your father are gone, now. I was very careful with them; but we'll soon be at their end."

Then I saw clearly the endless piecing together, the hard role that had been Maman's; a thousand memories seized me by the throat: Maman mending clothes of an evening under an inadequate light, absorbed in trying to save money, sending us to bed early so that the fire need not be kept up. "Under the covers, you don't feel the cold. . . ." And I recalled a hundred occasions when I might have helped her, whereas she packed me off to study a sonata. And how she would tell me: "You give me a great deal more pleasure, you know, by being the first in your class than by helping with the dishes." And once, when I insisted upon taking her place at the hand-operated washing machine, she had said to me, "If you really want to lighten my work, go play the "Moment Musical" while I go about my business. It's strange how that piece affects me; so gay, so airy, it drives all my weariness out the window!"

Yes, so it had been. But this evening I jumped from one extreme to the other. Now I ardently wanted to earn money. For Maman's sake, I think I even decided that I'd make a lot of it.

"Right off tomorrow," I declared to her, "I'll go look for work. No matter what! In a store, an office . . ."

"You in a store!" she exclaimed. "Besides, it requires some experience to sell things. No, there's no question of your earning a living at once, starting tomorrow, nor yet at haphazard. I can still keep you at your studies for another year."

And she told me what she wanted for me with all her heart: "If only you were willing, Christine, to become a teacher! . . . There is no finer profession, none more worthy, it seems to me, for a woman. . . ."

Maman had wanted to make all her daughters school-teachers – perhaps because she carried within herself, among so many shattered dreams, this lost vocation.

"It doesn't pay very well!"

"Oh! Don't talk like that. Should we value our lives by what we earn?"

"Since we must earn our livings, it's just as well to bargain for the highest price. . . ."

"Earn it, but not sell it," said Maman; "two very different things. Think it over, Christine. Nothing would please me more than to see you a teacher. And you would do wonderfully at it! Do think it over."

When as yet you scarcely know yourself, why should you not strive to realize the dream that those who love you have dreamed on your behalf? I finished my year at normal school, and then I went off to take my first school in one of our little prairie villages. It was a tiny little village, flat on its back, by which I mean really set flat upon the flatness, and almost entirely red in color; of that dark, dull redness you see on western railway stations. Probably the C.N.R. had sent paint. to cover the station and its small dependent buildings – the tool shed, the water tower, the handful of retired railway cars which served as lodging for the section foreman and his men. Some must have been left over, which the villagers had bought at a cut rate, or even got for nothing, and they had put it on all their walls – or at least that was what I had pictured to myself upon my first arrival. Even the grain elevator was red, even the house where I was to live, sheathed in sheets of tin several of which flapped in the breeze. Only the school had any individuality; it was all white. And that red village was called, still is called, Cardinal!

When she saw me, the lady with whom I was to board exclaimed, "Come, come! You're not the schoolteacher! Oh no; it's impossible!"

She adjusted her glasses to get a better look at me. "Why. they'll gobble you up in one mouthful!"

All through that first night I spent in Cardinal, the wind kept shaking the sheet metal that had come loose from this house, set off by itself on the outskirts of the village . . . but – it's true – escorted by two sad small trees, themselves, like it, shaken by the wind. They were almost the village's only trees; they became very precious to me, and later on I was most saddened when one of them was killed by the frost.

That first night, though, the wind spoke cruelly to me. Why was the village so atrociously red? Was it the color of its dreadful boredom? Certain people had warned me, "It's a village full of hatred; everyone hates some person or some object. . . ." Yes, but every village in our parts, even if it is red, even if it stands alone on the nakedness of the plain, always contains something more than hatred! . . .

The next day I crossed the whole village; truth to tell, there was but one long street, and it, in fact, was the public highway, a broad dirt road; and the village was so tiny a thing, so silent, that the highway passed through it at the same pace as it did the open country. I think that at every window someone stood to spy at me. Behind their curtains, could they have known what it is to set forth one morning along a wooden sidewalk that echoes your every step, in order, at the very opposite end of the suspicious village, to earn your living?

But since I had accepted the bargain, I wanted to live up to my end of it. "You give me so much in salary, I give you so many hours of work. . . ." No, it was not in that spirit that I wanted to do business with the village. I should give it all I could. And what would it give me in return? I did not know, but I gave it all my trust.

II

There were not many children that first day of school, and almost all of them very young. Everything went well. I began with geography; here was the subject I myself had liked best during my years as a student. It seems to me that geography is something that requires no effort, that you can't go wrong in teaching it, since it so captures your interest – perhaps because of the lovely big maps, each country indicated by a different color. And then it's not like history. In geography you don't have to judge peoples; no wars are involved, no sides need be taken. I spoke of the various crops raised in the different portions of the globe, in which regions grew sorghum, tapioca, bananas, oranges, sugar, molasses. . . . The children seemed delighted to learn whence came the things they liked best of all to eat. And I told them that they, too, in a sense labored for the happiness of others, since our Canadian wheat was known almost everywhere in the world and was very needful to sustain life.

When I returned, toward noon, to the house of red tin plate, Madame Toupin questioned me avidly. "Well? Did they eat you alive?"

Later on, Madame Toupin became my friend; since it was the one thing at which she best excelled, she was constantly reading my fortune in the cards. She foretold that I should travel a great deal, meet blond men, dark men. . . .

And indeed this is precisely what happened in very short order; on the Sunday following, a number of young men appeared at the sheet-metal house, in groups of four or five, who could not possibly all have come from nearby farms; some were from fairly distant villages. As the weather was fine, they sat themselves down upon a bench in front of the house. The spectacle of these boys in their Sunday best, sitting like bumps on a log, greatly astonished me, but, nothing daunted, I proceeded to take my walk, following the railroad right of way toward the little hills near Babcock. When I returned, rather late in the afternoon, the bench in front of the door was empty. Madame Toupin took me aside. "You're a strange girl," said she, "to leave your suitors flat like that. You are well liked for the moment, obviously enough; but if you continue to show your independence this way, it won't last; mark my words."

"What do you mean? Are those lads suitors of mine?" I asked Madame Toupin. "I never laid eyes on one of them before today, and why on earth did they all come in a group?"

"It gets around quickly in these parts," said Madame Toupin, "when a new schoolteacher comes to town, but I'm afraid that your distant manner has put your boy friends off for a long time. You'll certainly regret it this winter, for you'll have no one to take you to the parties. The boys have long memories around here."

"But what should I have done?"

"Sit down beside the boy who pleased you the most," replied Madame Toupin, "and thus make known your choice. Now I'm afraid it's too late to recover lost ground."

Other Sundays, being a little at loose ends, I began to cultivate the acquaintance, in one or another of the village houses, of its so shadowy people. The greater part of them became my friends, and practically everywhere the women got out their cards to tell my fortune. Ever since then I have clearly understood how much people stand in need of the novel, especially in a village like Cardinal, where new things almost never happen. Everything there was predictable: the preparations for sowing at certain set seasons, at others pure tedium. Then, too, the wind which sighed endlessly; even the monotonous pattern of dreams which the cards revealed.

Meanwhile, Madame Toupin had warned me, "Your trouble will begin when the older boys come to school. For the moment they are helping their parents with the threshing and fall plowing, but sometime in October you'll see the tough ones beginning to appear. I'm sorry for you, poor girl?"

Luckily they came one by one, which gave me the time to win them one by one . . . and in my heart I wonder whether these hard characters were not the more interesting. They forced me to be skillful, and to be just; they forced me to do many difficult things, true enough; they made me mount a tightrope, and once there, they never let me down. Everything had to be absorbing – arithmetic, catechism, grammar. A school without its rebels would be boresome indeed.

Thus the red village and myself were coming to know one another. Somehow I furnished it with a touch of that novelty which it loved above everything in the world, and it – I shall always remember – showed me the nobility of having to earn your living. And then winter fell upon us!

### III

How well I recall its brutal coming, along our highway! November was about to begin. The deep frost, the snow, all the pain of winter came in a single night along that shallow road. The wind urged them on with cries and ugly gusts. The next day we were snowbound. I had a very hard time beating my way through the drifts, often sinking above my knees. But I thought it fun to see the immense tracks I left behind me.

Of course there weren't many scholars in attendance that morning; in fact, by ten o'clock only the village children had put in an appearance. I imagine they had watched me going by their windows, and then that a number of them had thought of taking advantage of the trail I had opened. They had hastened to do so, for the wind quickly obliterated it.

But the farm children were nowhere to be seen. Used to thirty-five youngsters, I thought the dozen that now confronted me excessively well behaved, almost too docile. And when they had recited their lessons, when they had shown me their homework, what else was there left for me to do but tell them stories? For I knew I could have no illusions: often again would there be storms to keep the farm children from school. Were I to push the village pupils ahead, they would leave the others too far behind, and that could lead only to discouragement. In a way it was bitter to take advantage of the country children's absence and tell the others stories. But this, all the same, is what I did.

That day – so well do I remember it – we were as though cut off from the rest of the world in our warm little schoolhouse. In the cellar we had a big stove, and a register in the classroom floor. From time to time, one of my eldest students, lanky Eloi, would look at me, asking me a kind of silent question. I would nod at him. Then he would raise a trap door and climb down into the cellar to toss a few logs on the fire; shortly afterward the warmth would increase, while outdoors the driving snow seemed to fly even more violently. I toyed with the thought: "What fun to be shut up here with the children two or three days at a stretch, maybe even the whole winter! . . ."

I began, however, to miss those who were absent. I walked over to a window and tried to see in the distance, through the high whirling of the snow, the bit of path I had left behind in my passage; but at only a few feet from the building you could distinguish nothing.

Then, through the spirals of snow which seemed to climb in towers toward the sky, I suddenly descried something red – yes, two long scarves, their ends tossed in the wind, just as was the snow. It must be little Lucien and his sister Lucienne – by now I was well acquainted with the children's mufflers, and theirs were red. Their parents were from Brittany, having been at Cardinal for only five or six years, and they did not know how to read or write.

The two tots arrived almost frozen, their cheeks on fire. For prudence' sake, I rubbed their hands with fistfuls of snow; I helped them out of the coats that had stiffened over their bodies, and I kept them a little while standing on the register. Then they came to my desk with their readers and notebooks.

Later I learned that that morning they had made a great scene with their parents, who wanted to prevent their attempting the two miles on foot to school.

With me they were pliant. In their eyes, fixed upon mine, there was complete trust. I presume they would have believed me had I told them that the world was peopled with enemies, that they would have to cherish hatred for many men, even for whole peoples. . . .

But we – all of us together – were warm and happy. The two little ones recited their lessons. Right next to us the gale, like a misunderstood child, wept and stamped its feet outside the door. And I did not fully realize it yet – often our joys are slow in coming home to us – but I was living through one of the rarest happinesses of my life. Was not all the world a child? Were we not at the day's morning? . . .

## AFTERWORD

BY MIRIAM WADDINGTON

I never met Gabrielle Roy, but ever since I read and reviewed the stories in her *Street of Riches* back in 1958, I felt I knew her. The setting of her stories in the Winnipeg of the 1920s was the same setting I grew up in, although our family lived in a different part of Winnipeg – the North End on the other side of Roy's Provencher Bridge. Yet I knew St. Boniface, for the simple reason that we had to drive through it to get to St. Vital, where my father, a romantic Russian immigrant, had bought a twenty-six-acre farm to work in the evenings and on weekends. Our family sometimes visited a French-speaking family in St. Boniface, whom we had met one summer on a camping trip. And I had heard about the Saskatchewan Dukhobors from my father's conversations with one of his acquaintances who was writing a book about them. As for Eaton's, my mother and I were as familiar with its yard goods and remnants section as were Christine and her mother, for in those days most women out of necessity sewed for themselves and their children. And like Christine's, our family; and every other Winnipeg family as well, was horizon-bound so that every little creek, hillock, and chokecherry bush on the prairie felt like a gift from heaven.

Many years later, I read the opening words of Roy's auto-biography: "When did it first dawn on me that I was one of those people destined to be treated as inferiors in their own country?" And I realized that Roy was speaking for me and for every member of a minority group in Canada, and I blessed her for it.

In my review of *Street of Riches*, I said Roy's stories were magical. Coming to them again after all these years, I find them just as magical and far more moving. They still bring tears to my eyes, and not many books can do that for a reader like me who is burdened with a long history of reading as well as with the history of her own life and times.

So what did I find the second time around? I was impressed, first of all, with the wide range of Roy's interests and the variety of themes that emerge from these apparently simple stories about a family seen through the eyes of a child as she is growing up. Christine, the narrator, portrays not only her family, her street, and her neighbourhood, but a rich gallery of characters who, without even trying, are representative of the whole of Canadian society with its eccentricities, its charms, and its problems. With uncanny foresight Roy uncovers the social issues that have since emerged as the major problems plaguing us today. This is the darker, more shadowy side of her storytelling magic, and it is imperceptibly woven into what Henry James called the figure in the carpet.

Christine's family and friends are so individual and interesting that we are apt to overlook the significance that lies beyond and underneath the events in the stories.

What, then, are some of these significances, these figures in the carpet, that only a closer look can reveal? Let's take my favourite story, "The Gadabouts." It's about the human longing for freedom and the necessity to achieve it no matter what it costs. The story can also be read as a story about feminism, the eternal woman question, a housewife's attempt to declare her independence from husband, family, and domestic duties in order to fulfill her yearning for adventure in the outside world. Maman does this by creatively using the limited possibilities offered by her environment.

When Maman decides to travel to Quebec for a month, she is certain that her husband, who works for the Ministry of Colonization, will never allow the trip much less get her a railway pass. So she makes a plan. She boards two daughters in a convent and sends her son to boarding school. Then she goes to Eaton's, buys material and, working late into the night, sews two "travelling suits," one for herself and one for Christine. And how wonderfully loving is Roy's description of these creations! Still needing money, however, Maman puts on her suit and parades past the house of a richer neighbour who at once orders and pays for similar suits for herself and her daughter. With this money Maman buys tickets, leaves a note for her husband, and, taking her youngest child, Christine, goes off to Montreal to have adventures.

Once there, she visits her cousins and her husband's relatives and searches out her childhood friend Odile, now a nun in a convent. Christine observes everything closely: "I realized how much better received in society is a woman who boasts of her husband than one who is alone. This seemed to me unjust; I had never noticed that a man needed to talk of his wife in order to appear important." Maman also visits the shrine of Saint Anne de Beaupré, and Christine reports: "Kneeling in front of her statue, she had had a long talk with Saint Anne. I've always thought that what Maman then asked of her was to cure her forever of the need for freedom – perhaps not too promptly, giving her time for another trip or two. . . ."

Maman evidently feels guilty about her desire for freedom, for when they visit Saint Joseph's Oratory in Montreal, she asks Brother André "whether it was a great sin for a married woman to leave on a journey without having obtained her husband's consent." His reply is hasty and irrelevant: "Say a good prayer to Saint Joseph, don't drink too much coffee, and have trust, always have trust."

In the meeting with her childhood friend Odile, Maman expresses her doubts about freedom once more: "I sometimes wonder whether I go too far. . . ." But the wise nun replies, "There are many ways of obeying God, Eveline . . . and freedom is one of the roads on which to journey toward Him. . . ."

Maman's break for freedom does not seem so surprising when we hear her ideas about equality for women in her later conversation with a visiting older son in "The Jewels":

> When you come right down to it, there is no equality between men and women. The lovely virtues – loyalty, frankness, straightforwardness, admirable simplicity – you insist on for yourselves, whereas you esteem women for their wiles, their flightiness. And that's bad, first of all for yourselves, who are the first to suffer from it, and for women whom – it would seem – you enjoy keeping in a state of artful childishness. Oh, when . . . will the same qualities be of good repute for all! . . .

When Christine overhears these words, she immediately throws away her makeup, her perfumes, and her costume jewellery and decides then and there that she too wants equality.

Maman's notions about art are just as sound as her ideas about life. When Christine confides in "The Voice of the Pools" that she would like to be a writer and repay some of

the happiness books have given her, Maman is upset: "Writing
. . . is hard. . . . Is it not like cutting yourself in two, as it were
– one half trying to live, the other watching, weighing? . . ."
And she adds, "[Writing] is a very strange gift . . . not wholly
human. I think other people never forgive it." Yet, as Christine
affirms, "It was . . . her fault if I preferred fiction to daily life.
She had taught me the power of images." And indeed, the
stories are full of recurring images of trains, horizons, railway
tracks, the dark red of grain elevators, while the sound of
prairie winds and grasses conjures up the shifting moods of the
land, its people, and the infinite variety of both.

And it is in this variety that Roy's most important theme
is firmly embedded. That theme is the acceptance of differences, not just a tolerance for difference in others, but a
genuine understanding, sympathy and acceptance of that
difference. It is no accident that *Street of Riches* opens with
"The Two Negroes." In the 1920s what white family would
have taken a Negro as a boarder? On Rue Deschambault everyone always had money troubles, but Maman was the first to
take a Negro lodger. He was a porter who worked for the
C.P.R. along with one of her older children. Soon the neighbours acquired a second Negro lodger, and Christine tells how
"our Negro gave us lessons in kindness." He helped Maman
wind skeins of wool, paid for lessons in French from Christine,
listened to an older sister play the piano and went for walks
with her discussing Africa, and finally the two Negroes sang
harmonies to piano accompaniments by the daughters of
both families.

Christine also tells about the Italian labourer who came
every evening to work on the house he was building next to
theirs on Rue Deschambault. A recent immigrant, he could
scarcely speak either English or French; language, however,

did not interfere with the friendship between him and Christine's family. When his house was finally finished and his wife arrived from Milan, more neighbourly gestures were exchanged. Regrettably the Italian's life was cut short by an accident at work, but Maman long cherished the little wife's parting gift of a blue vase.

Then there was Wilhelm, a Dutch immigrant, who lodged nearby and became Christine's first suitor. Maman thought he was too old for Christine. Christine felt sorry for him: "He was an immigrant, and Papa had told me a hundred times that you could not have too much sympathy; too much consideration for the uprooted, who have surely suffered long enough from their expatriation without adding to it, through scorn or disdain."

The stories about Negroes, Italians, Dutchmen, Dukhobars, and Ruthenians are all charming and positive stories about one family's acceptance and understanding of people who came from different cultures and had very different beliefs. What lies underneath the stories, and is everywhere implied but nowhere directly stated, is that these differences were not so generally accepted in Canadian society, no more indeed than Christine's people were accepted when they went across the bridge to shop at Eaton's. This, then, is the figure in the carpet.

Maman and Papa were by no means average people. Although Maman was born in Manitoba, her father came from Acadian stock who settled in Quebec before coming to Manitoba. Papa was born in Quebec and had found his way to Manitoba after wanderings through the United States. The family was French but lived in a neighbourhood surrounded by O'Neills, Sarianos, and Jacksons as well as Guilberts. Partly because of Papa's work, partly because of their neighbours, partly because they themselves had felt the chill of discrimination, both parents understood what it meant to be an immigrant, a newcomer, or a homesteader.

At the same time both parents were securely rooted in their own religious and cultural identity and both had a sense of its continuity. When Maman returned from her journey to Quebec, she talked about her travels and reminisced contentedly, "the generations of the dead still breathe around the living in that ancient land of Quebec!"

Maman's striving for freedom and equality, appealing as it is, is nonetheless rooted in the opposite reality of women's lack of freedom and equality, just as Papa's love for his homesteaders is rooted in its opposite reality of the negative stereotyping by Canadian society of all minority cultures. These are the darker truths that fuel both the father's idealism and the mother's openness to new thoughts and unaccustomed ways. Maman reaches out for new experiences and learns something from each encounter. She is, as her childhood friend Odile says, one of those "beings set apart by Providence . . . set apart to their advantage."

And Gabrielle Roy, the writer, was another such a one. The book concludes: "Right next to us the gale, like a misunderstood child, wept and stamped its feet outside the door. And I did not fully realize it yet – and often our joys are slow in coming home to us – but I was living through one of the rarest happinesses of my life. Was not all the world a child? Were we not at the day's morning? . . ."

In spite of Maman's warning about the loneliness of a writer's life, Christine still hopes to have everything life offers: "a warm and true life, like a shelter – at times, too, unbeatable with harsh truth – and also time to capture its reverberations in the depths of the soul; time to walk, and time to halt that

I might understand; time to withhold myself a little along the road, and then to catch up with the others, to rejoin them and to cry joyously, 'Here I am. . . . Have you waited for me?'"

Christine did not need to ask. We have waited. And here they are, Christine and Gabrielle Roy, just as they wished it, forever alive in these pages.

# BY GABRIELLE ROY

AUTOBIOGRAPHY

La Détresse et l'enchantement
[Enchantment and Sorrow] (1984)

ESSAYS AND MEMORIES

Cet été qui chantait [Enchanted Summer] (1972)
Fragiles Lumières de la terre
[The Fragile Lights of Earth] (1978)
De quoi t'ennuies-tu, Eveline?
[What Are You Lonely For, Eveline?] (1982)

FICTION

Bonheur d'occasion [The Tin Flute] (1945)
La Petite Poule d'Eau
[Where Nests the Water Hen] (1950)
Alexandre Chenevert [The Cashier] (1954)
Rue Deschambault [Street of Riches] (1955)
La Montagne secrète [The Hidden Mountain] (1961)
La Route d'Altamont [The Road Past Altamont] (1966)
La Rivière sans repos [Windflower] (1970)
Un jardin au bout du monde [Garden in the Wind] (1975)
Ces enfants de ma vie [Children of My Heart] (1977)

FICTION FOR YOUNG ADULTS

Ma vache Bossie [My Cow Bossie] (1976)
Courte-Queue [Cliptail] (1979)
L'Espagnole et la Pékinoise
[The Tortoiseshell and the Pekinese] (1986)

LETTERS

Ma chère petite soeur: Lettres à Bernadette 1943–1970
[My Dearest Sister: Letters to Bernadette, 1943–1970]
[ed. François Ricard] (1988)